All rights reserved. No part of this publication may be reproduced, stored in a retrieval system, in any form or by any means without the prior written permission of the author, nor be otherwise circulated in any form of binding or cover other than that in which it is published and without similar condition being imposed on the subsequent purchaser.

All characters in this book are fictitious and any resemblance to real persons, living or dead, is purely coincidental.

Copyright Altany Craik 2020

In the Shadow of St Giles.
by
Altany Craik

Other Books in the series

Innocence Lost

For my Wife, who doesn't like horror stories but she puts up with me anyway.

Chapter 1

Hair is a strange thing. Why it holds on to a psychic impression I don't know but it does. In fact it sometimes works better than skin for my gift, it doesn't always but this time it does. The long hair I have in my fingers I picked off an iron fence that was thick with paint which was in the process of drying. It was waving there for me to find, catching the street light and screaming touch me.

Anyway, this hair, detached from the owner's head was like a full VCR replay without the snow and fuzzy bit at the top. The picture of the otherworlder's face (we are so politically correct these days, personally I call them demons) vivid and instantly frightening. The malice that it had exuded probably made this hair jump to escape. The deep black and red skin with sharp fangs would be enough to terrify most people. It had terrified her.

Somewhere around here it had struck. It was the third time. Somewhere around here a body would be found. Somewhere around here another memory highlight for the poor soul that discovers the body. I sigh, something I have being doing a lot these days. It seems to me that these events are coming closer together with fewer false alarms in between. Worse still, this is in Edinburgh where I live. Hiding in plain sight, or at least buried under the masses of people, it is effectively using the human noise to mask its presence and movements.

This one is a hard, slippery Bastard. Another name not in the Bishop's prescribed lexicon. I suppose I need to call him, the Bishop, not that he'll be worried about me. After all priests wandering darkened streets, at three in the morning, is so safe. Do I leave the call until the morning? A sane person would, I suppose.

Perhaps I will wait until I find the body and answer the awkward questions that the nice policemen will want answered. 'How did you come to be here at this time of night, sir?' I can almost hear it, the serious tone devoid of humour.

'I was following a hair.' Alice eat your heart out. Perhaps I will be able to think of an appropriate response, not including a swear word. I can feel her but not the demon. Her body is nearby, dead obviously, but very close.

In the labyrinth of the Old Town the shadows and secret places are many and well concealed. Under the Cowgate, and below the busier sections, is where my aimless wanderings have brought me. It has a certain smell, quite unlike anywhere else, old decay and laden with memories. Layer upon layer of events, detritus and vomit give texture and depth to the olfactory assault. Add now blood and demonic ejaculate and the platter of scents is complete.

Human brains do us a favour; they hide horrors to give us time to look away. Sadly, I have to look; it comes with the territory. The discarded torn body, half hidden under orange commercial refuse sacks, is a real treat. The spray shows up, to me, all over the walls of this alley and looks like an explosion in a paint factory. Luckily darkness will hide the worst from others for a while. The shredding of her flesh is the result of curved talons and an orgiastic frenzy and yet her face is untouched. It is contorted in agony but still recognisable, although all life has fled the scene. This poor girl was picked from a Friday night herd and taken. Her parents will be devastated, their grief adding to the tears of the world.

Another sigh and I am working my slightly numb fingers on my smartphone screen. Now that it is unlocked I need to choose; Bishop or police? Probably best to alert the Polis first. A few taps and I am through to a rather efficient operator.

'Can you wait until the Police arrive?' The female voice asks, no pressure implied. Do they get training to be non-threatening to witnesses?

'Of course.' It's not like I will be going anywhere, anytime soon. So many people call and leave, not wanting to be involved. I would probably be called anyway, cuts out the middle man.

'My name?' I respond caught a bit off guard. 'Father Steel, Andrew Steel.' Best bond voice and diction. I hang up, a little embarrassed at myself. This is no place for levity, something I often fail to recognise. Time to do my thing before I have any company and awkward questions.

A short prayer for the poor lost soul, whose body adorns this place, and I tip-toe through the puddles. I know that I will get a reaction and I ready myself. I touch her fingertips ever so lightly, giving me the chance to break the connection quickly if I should need to. The scream is like a sonic boom in my head causing me to jump away as her agony floods through me. Her last scream would have raised every house in the area. Why then did her passing go unnoticed? The psychic scream of Brenda Forth was like a red hot poker in my brain as I relived her last moments. The tears are sprinting across my cheeks and cascading onto the cold, dark stone. Another layer of pain laid on this psychic tapestry; not the first and probably not the last.

In the distance, and approaching fast, are the sirens. Utterly pointless now that the deed has been done. Waking up the neighbours for entertainment perhaps? The blue lights are soon bouncing off the alley walls; revealing and hiding the blood stains as they strobe round. The alley walls like the camouflage on the side of jeeps and trucks with the splatter patterns.

'Step away from the body, Sir.' Authoritative and polite; never knew it was possible. Aren't they getting younger these days? Fucked if I know.

I suppose I should be glad that it's not that cold and not raining as the young constable takes my statement. It is a long drawn out, pencil and paper, exercise. Full name, where was I born? Where do I live? Where was I going? It is this last one that stops the bus, as it were. Obviously he doesn't like my answer. Not really that surprising to me.

His brows furrow as he looks up from his little black book of tedious details. 'Sorry, where were you going at this time of night?' He repeats, changing my status in his head from body-finder to suspect. Small wonder that so few crimes are actually solved these days.

'I was coming here.' I know, I could have thought of something better but I have had enough with the charade.

'Why?' It gets out before he can stop it, his police face all confused.

'To find this.' I am being an unhelpful sod but it is late and I am bored now. He, on the other hand, is somewhat stunned. I dig out my wallet and extract my ID. God squad, my crime scene. I hand it to him and wait for the lights to come on.

'I'll get the Sergeant.' He manages and wanders a few steps away before realising I could wander off. 'Come with me, Father.' These city cops aren't too bad, it seems. I smile and tag along as he moves through the tape.

'Sarge?' He approaches tentatively. The Sarge looks like the one from Hong Kong Phooey – you know, a bit round and carrying his doughnuts in front of him.

'Yes?' Oh dear the walrus moustache makes him look fierce. My PC hands him my credentials, wordlessly. He obviously can't think of a better description than God Squad, either. I can almost hear the growl underneath the bushiest mouser I have seen in years. He gives me the 'I-have-seen-everything-now' look. He's not suitably impressed by me. What does he expect? Robes and the Spanish Inquisition?

He performs a perfunctory 'Check these out' over his radio-walkie-talkie thing. It doesn't take long for their authenticity to come back. His gruff look of disappointment is almost comical; I try not to laugh.

'Father Steel, Glad to have you. How can I help?' You could have knocked me over with a feather. He seems sincere too. This is not at all what I am used to. I usually find the territorial tendencies kick in and I am obstructed until I pull rank on the locals; Edinburgh it appears will be different.

'I will just try to stay out of your way, but we need

to see where the blood trail goes. He will have been covered in it.' Blinding statement of the obvious. Best if I keep the surprises to a minimum for now.

'Of course, SOCO will be here soon. We are canvassing the area for witnesses; someone will have heard something or if we are lucky, seen something.' He is so different from what I expected. He seems quite effective; a nice surprise at four in the morning.

'Excellent. Pretend I am not here.' I smile disarmingly, or at least I hope so.

'MacGregor. I am Sergeant MacGregor. I am sure the Inspector will want a word when he gets here. He's on his way.' I nod and shake the proffered hand. Two shakes, up and down and its over, like pissing in a public urinal.

I wander around like Inspector Clouseau but trying not to mess with the evidence. There is no real sign of a blood splattered trail leading away. Maybe in the daylight it will show up and that isn't all that long away. In my head I am rolling the VT of her last moments, horrible and vicious as it was, in the hope that I can glean something from reliving it. No streams of tears this time, fortunately. My grim set face seems to stop anyone from speaking directly to me but I overhear the little snippets 'Who is he? What is he doing here?' You know, the usual stuff.

Waiting for the Inspector is like waiting for a bus; no sign of one then two come along together. Actually one is a Chief Inspector and the other a Detective Inspector. The one with the shiny buttons is the Chief, apparently. The other one is in a crumpled overcoat. Oh my god, it's Rebus. I smile at my own, internalised, humour. Then wipe it off quickly as Chief Buttons approaches. He has been briefed it would appear.

'Father Steel, Chief Inspector Cushions. Terrible business.' I replay his words and find it was Cousins not cushions, would have been funnier my way. I nod and 'Rebus' sticks out a hand and nods. 'DI White.' He'll be the one doing the actual work.

'Good Morning, Don't let me get in the way.' I try self-deprecation as a way of getting them to bugger off while I think. This is the third murder in as many weeks and we are still fumbling about in the dark. This is the first time I have been on-site, as it were. There were no crimes against the church to call me to but I invited myself to this one. A few more pleasantries, card exchanges and I am left alone again, just watching and thinking.

Now the Brass and the Boss are here, order seems to spring from the chaos. Everyone knows their role and gets stuck in. The media, unshaven and rumpled are beyond the black and yellow tape that flaps gently in the breeze. I try to do my fade into the background act and I hope they haven't noticed me. Bishop Michael wants no questions yet.

Chief Inspector Cushions heads down to give a statement as SOCO and the Police doctor enter the alley from the other end. Thankfully there are no snappers trying to catch neither an explicit picture of the murder scene nor the mortal remains of Brenda Forth. For that I am sure her family will be truly thankful.

I am caught off guard by DI White when he hands me a polystyrene cup with dark liquid inside, I hope its coffee not something stronger.

'It's black. If you need milk and sugar you don't like coffee.' He smiles a genuine smile that reaches his eyes. He is a decent spud, apparently and quite young for a Detective Inspector, probably past thirty five but not by much.

'Thanks.' I take a sip and try to look cool, but it is

foul. 'Not that this is much like coffee.' White adds 'It's from McGregor's Thermos' He swigs and tolerates the foul taste. His eyes catch mine and hold them. He has The Question.

'Why are you here Father?' His voice is not a whisper but it does only reach my ears. He is discrete too, another blessing to be counted.

'To help.' I look over the white foam rim and see his face hardening, so I carry on, he deserves more 'Seriously, I am here to help. We need to stop these murders.' He isn't ready for the Big Truth yet.

'Well, we need all the help we can get. What do you think is going on?' He looks round the crime scene; he is keeping this between us.

'A vicious psychopath is cutting a swathe through the town and leaving very few clues. He is careful and yet the killings seem to be frenzied. Where's the blood?' Say nothing and yet seem to say a lot is a neat trick. I should be in politics.

'He's a careful psychopath then. These look random but something is niggling at me. No decent lines of enquiry are presenting themselves and the connections between the victims don't seem to exist.' His frustration is seeping out and that look, you know the seen-too-much look, has crept into his eyes. It happens and lurks around the eyes; a something that screams a pain in the soul that will never truly be washed away. Many cops get it; especially those that care and deal with murders, it makes them old before their time. DI White's salt and pepper hair is beginning to thin and his gut is hanging a little over his belt but he seems to command the respect of the uniforms at the scene. Like I said, he's a decent spud.

'A fresh pair of eyes maybe?' I hope it didn't come out as 'Let me do it.' I really need to think first and speak second. Oh well, too fucking late this time.

'Good idea.' He means it 'Meet me at the task force centre this afternoon and you can dig away.' And with that he's called away. Stunned, I sip the disgusting sludge in a cup. This might be a pleasure, not a struggle, working with the Edinburgh Polis.

Chapter 2

The Task Force Centre actually looks like one; you know desks, whiteboards, computers and cops running around like organised headless chickens. The Glossy pictures adorning the boards are a veritable collage of blood-splattered-TV-serial-killer-show-style scenes of carnage. Enough to make a hooker blush as they say or probably don't. I stand in the doorway, with my visitor badge on show, looking like a little lost sheep. Perhaps my hesitation is down to the lack of challenge or approach. I could be anybody.

I bimble with purpose over to the first board. Grizzly doesn't cover it. Grim probably does. The Victim's name is Annabelle Weston, that doesn't sound that local to me. It appears that I am right, she'd moved here from Manchester only last year. Discovered by the Bin men when they were doing the weekly uplift. No witnesses, no clues, no DNA and no chance. Slashed and eviscerated but no marks on her face. The look of terror will need brain bleach to remove it. A plethora of triplicate, typed forms cover the board and none of them are new. It seems the investigation has moved on to the next scene from serial killers 101.

I wander along, not quite aimlessly but, with an indefinite purpose. I have been to the next scene but the body had been removed by then. I saw the splatters and splashes of blood and they looked like a frenzy in the daylight; that was ten days ago. The home office pathologist report on the cause of death has stabbing in capital letters. I nearly snort derisively. I suppose disembowelled by demon claws wouldn't be in the drop down menu of choices. Massive blood loss incompatible with life in bold in the notes. You think? I shake my head at the lack of leads or viable lines of enquiry on this board. Drawing a blank would be overstating the progress. No witnesses on this one either. Not exactly the pattern I am looking for. Perhaps I need to touch the bodies? That will be a highlight to savour. The look of disgust must be showing as the 'worker ants' are beginning to notice my dog collar.

A WPC, if we are still allowed to call them that, approaches me. Just the right mix of 'Are you lost?' and 'Not another bloody brass visitor' covers here face. She opens her mouth and a clear concise and effective 'Good afternoon Father. DI White said you would be along' is

14

delivered. And she never said 'I thought you'd be older.' I smile gently, almost like she might expect. Play nice is my new motto.

'Good Afternoon, just leave me to it for now.' I don't want to waste her time nor let anyone in on the fact that I know as little as they do. I am meant to be a help, after all.

She nods and does just that; leaves me to it. Obviously she has real work to do. Across the office a ringing phone is answered by a rather spotty, dishevelled young man not in a uniform.

'DC MacBride.' He rasps into the receiver. I can't believe he is a detective; he looks about twelve years old. The face he pulls as he tastes the, apparently very cold, contents of his mug tells a story. The coffee here is disgusting. I smile at his discomfort and turn away before anyone notices. This is not a place for levity.

Reading police-speak reports is a tiring pastime and I have persevered much longer than I usually do. The manilla folders have moved from one pile to a new one as I plodded my way through them. Witnesses are very thin on the ground and are proving that they saw and heard not very much. Only one nags at me and not because it comes from a prostitute. Her witness statement has a reference to being cold and uneasy. A possible lead for me, not much use to the polis though. I make a note of her name and address and her working handle too, well you never know when you will need something like that. A prostitute called Tiffany, sounds so much more exotic than Carol MacDougall.

'Tea Father?' The WPC is back and seems at ease with my presence. I smile again, getting the hang of playing nice.

'Call me Andrew.' I take the red mug catching sight of the 'keep calm and carry on' logo; so very apt for this place.

'PC Craig, Jill.' She smiles back and I notice her lovely eyes. She is pretty but she looks about twelve too. They are getting younger these days. It isn't my imagination.

'When will DI White be back?' Not that I really need him but I will want to talk to him now that I am up to speed on the pointless reports.

'He will be in around six. Is there anything I can help with?' She hooks a wayward lock of brown hair behind her left ear. It is an unconscious thing and probably takes place twenty times an hour.

'I need to see the bodies. Can you arrange it?' It is a matter of fact delivery and I offer no explanation as to why. She seems unfazed, as if expecting unusual requests from me. After all how many priests are included in a multiple murder investigation?

'Of course, I can take you over to the morgue after your tea if you'd like? I just need to make a call.' I nod and soon I will be off to a harrowing event, oh the joys of my life.

'Annabelle Weston.' The orderly pronounces as he pulls out the tray. The cold air rolls out like Dracula's fog. The ruination of her torso is profound and, although tidied up, is still shocking in the severity of the wounds. Her blonde hair has lost its shine and clings limply to her head. Thankfully, the terror has faded from her features, her face is slack and betrays none of the trauma she suffered. I let my fingers trace along her forehead. My audience seem scandalised that I am touching the body.

A rapier thrust of visions lances into my brain like a scalding. Almost instantly I need to be away from contact. I am hearing her screams and feeling the lacerations as they were being inflicted. Vivid, almost a re-enacting, I break contact and stumble away. The pains in my gut I know are echoes but they feel very real to my brain and I collapse in a heap. I would say I was writhing but more like a contortionist explosion as I rub my chest.

'Are you all right Father?' They are in my face, all concerned and worried. My body is bathed in sweat that has miraculously coated me in seconds. I manage to pull air into my lungs. To their stares I expect I look like a landed fish. The gulping is steadying my breathing and I manage to croak 'I'm fine.' After all, doesn't everyone throw themselves on the ground after touching a body? They don't seem to believe me, if the looks on their faces are anything to go by.

Her, Annabelle's, experience was viciousness incarnate but more than that was the undercurrent of sexual gratification. The demon had taken her; keeping her alive and conscious as his barbed, engorged phallus ripped up into her insides. I could feel my gorge rising as I began to relive and feel the tearing in my gut. Luckily I was able to shut down the feelings and keep the contents of my stomach from presenting themselves all over the floor. A plastic cup is being thrust into my hand, and directions to drink are beginning to intrude on my brain. I drink it and sit for a moment; you know, recovering as if anyone really recovers from this.

'Why is there no mention of sexual trauma in the notes?' I fire out from left field. Their faces, at another time might be comical, are shocked. Apparently it was a secret. Not from me it wasn't.

'We haven't ascertained what caused the damage to

her. It is almost like a medieval torture piece was used.' PC Craig manages to mumble out, her young features still not covering the shock she has held in about it.

'I see.' I don't feel the need to expand further. A little mystery never goes amiss. Anyway I need to get outside and I let Annabelle Weston's memories slip away for now. Memories that will lead me to her killer. No one gets away with this.

From her eyes, as she was torn and shredded, I caught a glimpse of where it killed her. Not where she was dumped but where it did the deed. Unluckily for the Demon I recognise the place. His trail may be cold but it isn't gone. I am coming and he won't enjoy that.

Chapter 3

'So Father, Jill tells me we had an episode at the morgue.' DI White, it seems, is a master of understatement. He doesn't seem too happy either. I thought he was going to be all right, too. I am sure the disappointment wont kill me.

'You might call it that; I couldn't possibly comment.' A Sir Humphrey response. I am being childish but I have an excuse. I can still feel the ache in my gut from having my womb ruptured. Oh wait, I don't have one; so why do I still ache?

'Talk to me Father Steel. What do I need to know?' Maybe he'll be okay after all. Maybe he's getting heat from above, now is the time I suppose. I sigh.

'DI White, I am going to tell you something. Something difficult to believe but is true none the less.' I pause for effect. His eyes have narrowed as his suspicion is writ large on his face. He doesn't interrupt, however.

'You know that I represent the Church and the

Home Office.' He nods, unsure of where I am going. His face is schooled almost as if he has to regularly hide his thinking.

'This is covered by the Official Secrets Act and disclosing the things I tell you will result in prosecution and imprisonment.' I use my serious adult voice. The blue twinkle in his eyes is excitement not psychosis, I hope. He waits, leaning forward slightly.

'I am a psychic. When there are crimes that need my gifts I am sent to resolve them. Your murders need my gifts. Our murderer is a demon.' I wait for a beat. His breathing is steady and he seems to accept what I am saying.

'However, we can hardly go on the news with that.' I smile gently. Usually the recipient of my statement babbles a bit. Some times they have an explosive denial and outburst. DI white just soaked it up.

'So what happened in the morgue?' Damn he's good. No wasted questions; just right in. Damn, I like him.

'I touched the body and I got a full replay of her passing. It wasn't pleasant.' He nods as if he understands, Bless him. 'I get to feel it too.' He winces in sympathy earning some brownie points with me.

'I did get a lead, though.' I produce my rabbit from my proverbial hat. Although, to be honest, it's a very small rabbit and Edinburgh is a very big hat.

'This one?' DI white asks, hopefully. It's only the fifth set of flats that look exactly like the view I got. I shrug. It might be but, then again, I thought the last two were definitely right. We press the trades button and I let DI White push. The wave of psychic power that washes over us is intense causing me to stagger back. There is a sweeter smell too.

'This is it.' I manage to choke out a few words. My mouth is filling with saliva and my stomach is giving petite-lurches wanting to join in. I really don't want to hurl right now, not after the morgue performance. I want DI White to respect me in the morning. Why? I have no idea but I still do.

'Smells a bit fruity.' White sniffs the air. A penlight comes out and the super-strong cone of white light reveals a very dirty stairwell filled with detritus. The residents, apparently, don't seem to mind.

'Upstairs.' I step inside letting the magnetic door catch seal us in. The click-clunk feels like a prison cell door locking out the real world and keeping us in. The delights of a murder scene await us upstairs. The concrete stairs deaden the sounds of our footfall. Six floors up our prize lies. We pass a number of steel covered doors with polythene bags taped to them, inside there are papers.

'Evictions.' White tells me over his shoulder. I didn't ask, but thanks anyway. I trudge along trying not to wheeze. I need to do more exercise, I promise myself I will remember. The seminary has a gym of sorts that I have never used nor seen totally at odds with the current health and well being agenda that the Bishop is promoting.

'No wonder no one noticed. Are there actually any residents in this block?' I speak quietly and yet it still seems to ring out loudly. There are three doors on each landing and finally we stand outside our goal. My knees are giving me a warning that this type of activity should be avoided in future. I nod in response to DI White's look. It is this one and I can almost hear the screams of terror. She could have been screaming her pretty lungs out and no-one was here to hear her. I shake my head feeling her despair, trying to dispel it.

DI White turns the handle and sets his shoulder to the door. It groans as he snowploughs the crap on the other side. His light shines over a dry smeary trail of blood that coats, in nearly-dry splatters, the uncarpeted floorboards of the hall. The door to the living room has partially fallen off one hinge and the red rusty dots of blood clash with the old-nicotene-darkened orange gloss.

'Watch where you step.' White steps forward, carefully placing his feet. Of course, now I can't see what I am standing in. That is the least of my worries as the psychic screaming and demonic presence that once filled the hall are battering at my brain. I stand still; it's about all I can do without staggering. White murmurs into his radio, I presume he is calling this in. No doubt we will need to preserve the scene as they say on all those American detective dramas.

I flick the grimy light switch and, amazingly, the lights come on courtesy of Osram and the electricity board. I instantly wish I hadn't. I survey dirt and mess of frequent four-legged visitors apparent among the shredded take-away rubbish. The appetiser over the main course is yet to be revealed in, what was once, a living room.

The sofa, probably one of Ikea's finest, is against the near wall, an island of very dirty beige. A big red pool stain filling the middle cushion and more totally destroying the Swedish elegance and design. I scrunch my eyes closed to dispel the picture that confronts me, knowing that DI White cannot see the scene as it once was. A geometric, nylon based, seventies pattern carpet has soaked up some more of the liquids that her evisceration provided. Was the poor girl taken in her own home? A place where she should have been safe. How had it gotten in and why would be mysteries that we might never fathom. Although looking round, it is very hard to believe that this is anyone's home. A flop zone of desperation would be a more apt description. The waves of despair lying under the terror like undertones of a good wine are seeping into me and I try to keep the tears on the inside of my eyelids.

'This is where she was killed.' Someone has to state the obvious. I am not touching anything if I can help it. I don't want to re-live this again, the ache in my insides only recently forgotten. I need to remove some of the emotional charge in this room so that I can function. At the moment the maelstrom of memories blowing round me is making thinking and breathing a multi task too far. I start to dispel the energy in the room. It sounds like muttering but the words of Our Lord are incredibly powerful things.

The darkness of the room is lifted a little as I push away her pain and the debilitating terror. Her soul escaped from the torment of her flesh at the time but the echoes of her hurt remained until now.

The layers of despair that imbue this room are a problem for another day. I can now breathe and keep my eyes open; progress I think. My cheeks are damp, coated with my tears, remnants of the emotions I have just endured. The whole block holds more painful memories than any one place should have to bear. The waves of unhappiness, desolation and fear have been laid down by tenant after tenant. Grinding poverty and generations of lives devoid of hope have created this black pit. Did this attract the Demon? It's a theory.

'Was this her address?' I fire my question out of the blue as White does his cop poking around. Looking over his shoulder 'No she lived in Stockbridge somewhere.' He gives me an answer that helps and just raises more questions.

'A bit of a trek over here then eh?' An unspoken someone, or many some-ones, must have seen something. An appeal maybe? Might be worth a try anyway. How is this bastard able to move about unseen? Red skin, horns, claws and fangs are usually noteworthy.

The smell, at once unique and overpowering, fades after a few minutes until it is hardly really noticed. It's a bit like dog owners with the wet-dog smell. They don't seem to mind while we cat-people want to gag.

I decide to leave DI White to poke around until his heart's content. I will have a wander around. From here I should be able to follow our other-world visitor (the lexicon of political correctness) he will leave a very singular trail; a joy that will be, no doubt.

In less than forty-five minutes the white-suited, humour-bypassed mob arrive. The crime scene tapes a barrier to the other residential ghouls. I am allowed an access-all-areas-backstage pass. Uniform are on the stairs. While standing usefully about I wonder if Chief Inspector Buttons will make an appearance. A bit like the pantomime Dame, I snort as the Widow Twankie look fills my imagination. The radio bleeping and static are giving me a headache or perhaps it is the demon mojo and the smell. I make my way onto the landing, ducking under the yellow and black tape like a veteran.

The trail, which was the reason for this excursion leads me downstairs. It is not new but now I can pick it out from the many other trails running over it; psychic bloodhound, that's me. The visit here seems like a one-off; not a habitual. At least I can only find one path to follow. Passing through the magnetic-lock door and reaching the clean air of the city, I suck in a great dollop. Urchins, hanging on the railings, are watching everything all excited and wide eyed. A muddy football, tucked under an arm, unable to compete with a murder. Personally, I blame TV. It makes excitement of tragedy; shows out of misery and shit programs out of good books.

The gaggle of whispering, nudges and staring at me as a result of my dog-collar seems to reach a frenzy among these unwashed little oiks. I make my way over to them and I swear they have stopped breathing.

'Awright boys? You from round here?' I pretend I like kids. I don't really though. They nod; it's a start I suppose. 'Seen anyone who shouldn't be here hanging around?' I ask gently, all cool like, with no inquisitional pressure.

'Are you wi' the pigs mister?' Oh the mouths of babes, revealing the worst of what they hear.

'It's Father and yes I am.' I smile as the gang tell Wullie to shut up. They might get in trouble. 'Did you see someone Wullie?' Kids aren't born bad, they just learn real quick round here. He shakes his head a little too vigorously to my way of thinking. He doesn't want to be a grass, I suppose.

I wear my gentle persuasion face, all friendly and Holy. I smile and get down to their level; on my hunkers. 'It's okay to tell me; they'll no bother.' I twitch my head in the direction of the uniform standing at the door. 'What did you see?' I pause. They might give up their information without the need for a bribe. The bumping and nudging continues as Wullie is prompted to 'spit it oot'.

'Ah saw sumfin.' Sniff 'It wiz getting dark and a big man came oot the flats and walked up the road. He walked funny.' Wullie had described every drunk and Jakey in Edinburgh.

'What was he wearing?' I try to tease out

something useful from this illuminating interaction. Wullie, it seems, is on a roll, and there is no stopping him now.

'A big coat like him.' The dirt filled fingernail at the end of his grimy hand, catches my attention and I see that he is pointing at a Mac, worn by one of the many functionaries at the crime scene.

'Tell him about the smell.' One of the prompters whispers. No detail too small in this story that won't bear the retelling.

Wullie, struggling for vocabulary, blurts it out 'He wiz stinkin, like a dead cat.' Fingers plugging his nose as he recalled the smell, the gang all giggle at the pantomime.

'Thanks Wullie. Here, get yersels a sweetie.' I put a fiver in his grimy little paw. In the old days it was a few coins; that's inflation for you. I open myself to see if I can get an image of the Mac-wearing, funny-walking smelly suspect. My fingers bump Wullie's hand and I glean a clear, if somewhat fleeting, image to hold on to. Thank you my boy, you have been more than helpful.

DI White is a good guy to know. He has a few

strings pulled and within twenty minutes a sketch artist is sitting with me in the back of a police transit van pulling the face of our suspect together. Obviously, I am describing young William's image not the demonic form that I am more familiar with.

'How's that Father?' The question catches me off guard a little as he turns it round. My eyes widen at the very lifelike depiction. It is incredible. 'Bang on' as they say.

'It is excellent, very much like our guy. We should show it to DI White and get it on the news.' The start of a plan forming inside my, usually empty, head.

After all if we make out that the suspect is a mass-murdering psychopath, the good people of Edinburgh might just spot him. It would certainly hamper his movements at any rate. DI white, as if in response to my thought, slides open the side door and climbs in. Outside, it is beginning to rain; a real surprise I don't think. He nods approval at the likeness and smiles a bit ruefully.

'David Gilroy.' He motions to the picture. 'I found a drivers licence upstairs. The sketch is very good, though.' He pulls an evidence bag from his pocket. There on the pink and white plastic is our man.

31

'Let's get him on the news.' DI White is looking forward to having a lead at last. Can't say I blame him. My way was better, though.

Chapter 4

I just need a deerstalker and a magnifying glass and my transformation to Basil Rathbone will be complete. I don't have a bumbling, portly Watson to look smart next to but I make do with a succession of modern Lestrades. A city is a wonderful place; full of mundane and mysterious places. Edinburgh is old and, to my sensitivities, a great many supernatural echoes are cast over its streets. It makes my blood hounding a little bit difficult at times. My demon has a head start so I might need a while. DI White is busy processing the scene and reporting up the chain of command. I suppose I should do the same but it can wait. Oh what a rebel I am.

You have to wonder about the people who designed these housing estates; they are a cluttered mess of curves and boxes. The houses like rabbit hutches and all in need of a good scrub, some of the gardens are nice though. Depressing cheek by jowl, crushed-in living and there is just no space to be. The resident's cars fill the streets on both sides almost to capacity. This working class area is not the modern, uplifting, post war utopia that was expected or promised. The Council can't even keep the weeds from the verges and cracks in the pavement. It is a demoralising mess.

It has been about ten minutes since I was certain that I had a trail to follow so now I am reduced to scanning from side to side like some sort of metal detector. Beep, Beep, Beep no psychic trail, Beep, Beep Beep. I must look like a bloomin' arsehole scanning the ground for coins. Not been mugged yet, so all good I suppose.

The reputation of this scheme is well known and not a good one. So no self-respecting human being should be wandering here once the sun goes down. Here I am, anyway, I am sure my dog collar will protect me. The orange street lights are coming on like an early warning system telling the non-local denizens to hurry up and leave. I am tough, so any hints are a waste of time. These mean streets are no tougher than the ones of my childhood. Aye, right.

It is getting properly dark and I have lost contact with the trail, so backtracking will be needed. That will need to wait as I need a pee. A middle-aged man issue that has made me an expert in finding a loo almost anywhere. I try not to think about it. Whistling helps, no really it does. So tunelessly I am keeping a tune going as I make my way along the less than friendly streets.

My pit stop is just around the corner. St Sebastian's Church; a modern utility space with toilets and thankfully it is open to the world most of the time and tonight is no exception. The minister does a great job with the dispossessed in his patch, you know, God's mission and all that. Buggered if I can remember his name; face yes, name no. Good job it is on the sign on the outside, written in nice gold lettering.

'Father Andrew, so lovely to see you.' His twinkling eyes, above a broad grin is, so sincere it is disgusting. I am conscious that my hands are damp after a lack of paper towels in his facilities. I wave as I cross the vestibule, ruefully trying to indicate my hands are not dry. He grabs one and shakes it anyway.

'How are you? I was nearby and needed to make a little visit to the boy's room.' I laugh no point in pretending otherwise. Honesty is the best policy is what we are all taught as children and forget as puberty strikes.

'We are a haven for those in most need. Glad to have been here for you.' His voice is a rich beast that probably sounds fantastic from his pulpit. He even looks godly; his hair has just the right mix of salt and pepper and good looks. His congregation will love him, I have no doubt. If Carlsberg did Men of God, this is what they would come up with.

'What brings you here, apart from our facilities?' It is the most normal question in the world and I need to think quickly. Of course, he has no idea what I actually do and probably thinks I am a scholar or something.

'I am helping the police with some specialist knowledge support in their murder cases.' Nearly the truth and a pretty good 'don't ask any more because I am not able to tell you' response.

'That sounds fascinating. You must be kept very busy.' He is ushering me into his office and away from the exit. The group therapy people in his church hall need their privacy and he ensures that.

'It is all the excitement I can take and more.' I do self-deprecation and a rueful face. I am crap at small talk and sometimes conversations end up being interrogations or strained silences. Father Peter plays mother with the tea and it is obvious to me he wants to say something; perceptive or what?

'I have a few very worried young ladies in my flock. They are terrified about this serial killer in Edinburgh.' He looks over his cup as he sips. Perhaps he knows something useful.

'It is terrible. Surprising that there have been no witnesses coming forward.' That's me, Say Nothing Steel. A funny look settles on his face, not funny ha-ha more funny contemplative. Almost as if he's not sure how to put it.

'Some of the girls have been telling me about a strange guy that has a funny walk and smells a bit rotten.' He just blurts it out. Can I play him at poker on pay day? He'd lose the lot. He has just blurted out our only lead. 'And they are keeping off the streets. Might not be a bad thing all the same.'

He's worried and he needed someone to tell. I was his someone apparently. There's more to come but he won't be using the big E word. Evil. We hardly say that these days. Oh if only he knew the half of it; Evil would be every other word he used.

'Where does this guy hang out?' I might as well ask , you never know. When serendipity takes me somewhere unexpected there's always a reason. I like to let it play out. Great process isn't it; if it ain't broke and all that.

'They keep seeing him down by the old community centre. It has been shut for years and is all boarded up.' Father Peter paused and swigged his tea. Mine's cold, so his must be too. The silence begins; he is trying to let it out.

'He sounds like our person of interest. I will get the police to check him out.' Listen to me all technical and official. What I really mean is that I will take a look and fumble about. If it is my guy it will probably be better that I just deal with it. I smile reassuringly.

'Of course he might just be some weirdo that creeps everyone out.' I add putting my unfinished cup on the table. I am not drinking cold tea on purpose, there are limits; cold coffee yes, tea no.

'I went to find him.' Here we go; more serendipitous clues falling into my lap from on high. I wait; not quite on the edge of my seat but I want to tell him to 'spit it out!'

'You know, to see what help I could get him. We

have a great homeless program in the capital. Lost sheep and all that.' He's a little embarrassed at doing the right thing. Maybe it is I that should be feeling ashamed at my lack of pastoral focus.

'Anyway, I went to the community centre and didn't go in. The boarding has been opened up I think.' Father Peter has been looking at the wall as he spoke but now his eyes have caught mine. 'I was too scared to go in. Really terrified.' His words are almost hissed and his eyes are staring hard. 'I have never felt such dread, ever.' There, it's now out in the open.

Father Peter has stumbled upon my Demon's lair and is sensitive enough to feel and fear its presence. If he had wandered in I might have been looking at his corpse in the morgue. I look deeply at him, he'll do. I smile, gently. Help unexpected is a little miracle all on its own.

'Let us go together and we shall see what we see. When two or three are gathered together in my name, I am with them. The Lord will be with us.' I let my calming spirit roll over him and can see him visibly bolster. I imagine it like a little blue wave washing away fear and bringing calm.

'Father Andrew, I feel so silly.' He begins but I

stop him. I give him a reassuring smile, I hope. His eyes have lost that wildness that was there only a few moments ago.

'No Father, when the Lord warns us, we must listen. Let us go now and see.' I am trying to get the tone right; firm but not mental. Usually comes out with psychotic undertones. He nods, accepting the call to arms with no further resistance.

A few minutes later we are a couple of middle aged priests wandering along the road. The rain has started and will just add to the experience. To the rest of the world all is fine but inside my head why can I hear the theme from the exorcist. We move through the raindrops and the pools of the orange street lights.

Chapter 5

Gordonstoun, this housing scheme obviously named after the school of royal patronage, is a utilitarian place reminiscent of the seventies films by Ken Loach. Depressing and dull you might call it; I couldn't possibly comment. The render is painted an off white and I am sure that helps break up the monotony. The street lights and drizzle just complete the picture and feel of misery. Joy seems like a very unlikely visitor to these streets.

Father Peter is tour-guiding all the way to our destination. So and so lives there, he had a heart attack last year. Mrs McBlah lives here, lost her son in Iraq. And on it goes; I'm not really listening. I can feel a growing pressure, an unease. We are definitely going to be having an event. The trail is like a shining ribbon of pain and dark despair. That might just be an echo of years of post-Thatcherite worklessness that has blighted too many communities in central Scotland. It's all her fault obviously. At least so the politicians keep on saying, and for once they might be right. Broken clocks are right twice a day so it shouldn't be too surprising if they luck out.

The hedges round here are bushy, vigorous beasts that encroach the footpaths giving a claustrophobic feel at best and cover for thugs at worst. Damp but undaunted we turn into Something street; I am sure it has a name but 'street' is all that remains of the sign fixed to the side of the houses. At the end, in the midst of some greenery sits the flat-roofed dereliction that is the John Thompson Community Centre. Named after the Celtic goalie, apparently.

Boarded up to keep the 'yoof' out; the sterling board panels have been adjusted to allow access to anyone who really wants in. Father Peter pauses as we pass the sign forbidding entry. I can feel the laid down dread, it would keep most folks away. They might not know why but they would not choose to go any closer. Well those with no God inside might not feel anything and stumble inside.

'Walk with me Brother.' My tone has changed. It happens when I stop being me and act like the messenger of the Lord I am. I expect him to follow as I move up the crumbling tarmac path. Perhaps I should have started a hymn; something uplifting. I feel my lips twitch at my own humour, but the near smile dies as I start to smell the decay that is our particular 'friend' from the hells.

The way in, of which there are a few, is well used and I probably could have found it anyway. Father Peter is tight lipped and anxious. He seems to be inching behind me, more and more. The board is loosely attached and can be encouraged to open with very little effort. The cavernous black hole that kills any light is like the throat of the beast. Inside, out of the rain, a darkness of more depth than is possible awaits us.

'Follow me.' I cross the threshold. If Peter crosses behind me, he is a brave man. He does and behind us the night is shut out. The immediate lack of the rain noise makes the silence loud in our ears.

'Let there be light.' The click of my mag-lite torch brings a white, clean cone to drive out the darkness. I try not to smirk but I know I am. 'Chocks away!' I might as well have said.

Where once there had been carpet tiles now only the outlines of old glue make the pattern. We have entered through a side entrance and the corridor leads ahead of us with doors to either side. Offices and toilets or changing rooms: I have no idea but behind any one of them a nasty surprise could be waiting. I stand for a moment just soaking in the silence waiting for my equilibrium to return when the rich baritone of Father Peter sounds out a wakey-wakey.

'Hello!' He calls out. I try not to jump in surprise and fail miserably. Of course, it could have been worse had the effeminate squeak had escaped my lips. Is he expecting an answer? Might as well have rung the bell or booted in the front doors. There are reasons I prefer to work alone. Fucks sake.

Going by the empty Buckfast bottles and chip wrappers, this has been a favourite haunt of kids for a while. As we begin our advance I can feel the air thickening ahead of us. It's a bit like wading through soup. Behind me, Father Peter's footfalls sound much less assured. I press on. He must follow or be left in the dark. If he is feeling half of what I am he won't want to wait in the dark. He's keeping up.

The swing doors with glass circles, so loved by councils everywhere, are slightly ajar. Hinges jammed or broken, I have no idea. My white cone fills the space and sends a little light beyond. I peek inside and lightly push open the one on the left. A deep breath, filling my lungs with stench, was not a good idea. I cough and my eyes are watering leaving me temporarily vulnerable. Father Peter fills the corridor with the contents of his stomach. His retching, almost, encourages me to join in.

The sudden scuff-scuff and thumping footsteps means we have company. That company is charging at us with murder in mind. I can hear its spite clawing through the air at us. Shit.

Fighting in the dark is terrifying but fighting in the strobe of a waggled torch is even more so. You can see just enough to be terrified and not enough to do anything about it. Who's idea was this anyway?

The bellowing roar as the demon charges elicits a terror-filled scream and not from me.

Father Peter has seen enough in the torchlight to be properly unmanned. The thumping impact of a hard shoulder bowls me into a breeze-block wall; the cement unforgiving as I bash my skull. Seeing stars might be one description; agony might be another. In the fall I have released our only light; it casts a spinning disc of white across the floor like a seventies disco revealing the detritus and little strewn floor.

Father Peter has stopped screaming and it takes me a moment to realise why. Two hands wrapped around his throat are choking the life from him. I suppose I should be thankful, our enemy is still inside the human cadaver and not in its true form. Otherwise Peter's throat would have been ripped out already and he could have been on his way to Saint Peter.

Getting to my feet is a struggle but I manage it. Waves of nausea roll over me, worse than any whisky fuelled sickness. The dizziness is good though, people pay good money for this sensation. I wobble forward with my crucifix ahead of me. I lumber into the beast with two backs rolling on the floor.

Contact with our foe is like a huge static charge running over my skin but when my blessed crucifix hits home the surge of power is like holding bare wires. We are catapulted apart, Father Peter lying between us. A howl of pain-filled anger fills my ears as it escapes up the hall and away. All my energy gone, I slump down next to Peter. Remarkably, he is still with us. Groaning and gasping like a landed fish but still in the land of the living. Tears are running down his cheeks but I don't think he cares about that, though. His throat is all crushed, bruised and scratched but he'll live. He won't ever be the same again but he'll get over it, probably.

'Fuck.' The ubiquitous expletive is so apt at this moment. Peter nods, seems we agree on that then. I let out a long held breath that comes out in shuddering little gasps. I pull out my mobile and call the Polis. They will have to come in and get us, I am walking nowhere at the moment. I am sure DI white won't be happy that I went out to play without him. Anyway in the meantime Father Peter and I need to have 'The Talk' and get our stories straight.

They're no very quick, these Edinburgh Polis. Where else would an attempted murder take twenty minutes to get to? Maybe I shouldn't have said the attacker was gone. Perhaps a 'he might still be here' would have worked better. The rewards of honesty are, as usual, piss poor. Dropping DI White's name obviously made no difference either. After a protracted wait they are arriving; better late than never but heigh-ho.

Armed response officers make a hell of a racket as they cleared their way down the hall. High-power torches blind us poor victims as we put our hands up to block them out. We are like a pair of priestly vampires caught in the light. I need to get one of theirs, puts my mag-lite to shame.

'Father Steel. Father Steel are you alright?' What impeccable manners too!

'I'm fine he's gone.' I manage to make myself held over the noise. 'Father Peter needs the paramedics. Where's DI white?' I go into frustrated cop, TV cop mode, barking out orders. I don't think they are paying a blind bit of notice though.

Being assisted to your feet like a pair of old codgers is a bit much but they mean well. In a few quick heartbeats we are in the back of an ambulance being quizzed, questioned and poked.

DI White arrives just in time. He has headed off an outburst of irritation after my being asked the same question for the third time. 'Did I get my name wrong the last twice?' I snap.

'Father Steel. Thank goodness you are all right.' He climbs in beside us. Father Peter is being helped further into the ambulance. The paramedic is taking my blood pressure again. He seems concerned about something. His machine keeps bleeping and the screen resetting or whatever.

'I hit my head, by the way, you know the bit that's bleeding.' I try to be helpful but it is coming out like a diva.

DI white laughs 'barely a scratch.' It seems the paramedic has had the humour bypass and gives me the shut up look.

'I know but your blood pressure is very high.' He knows he's dealing with a child. So fucking what I want to say but manage to keep it in. I roll my eyes and White thinks it's mildly amusing. With friends like him, I see why monasteries are so popular.

'We need to go, Sir.' He speaks directly to White. It seems that when you are hurt you are no longer in charge of yourself. Still here.

'DI White, it was our guy. He can't be too far away. He's been hiding in there.' I pause as he starts getting out. Where the fuck is he going?

'I will come to the hospital as soon as I can.' He shuts the door and with a double thump we are off.

I lie back on the gurney thing as Instructed. Resistance is futile, it seems. I let my eyes close for just a minute. I am knackered.

Chapter 6

I was only out for a moment, honest. Well probably a wee bit longer than that but the persistent 'Father Steel can you hear me?' is bloody annoying and eventually I felt compelled to open my eyes and reply.

'Yes.' I managed without the attendant 'Now fuck off!' The sound of relief floods through her voice

'We'll be taking you for an X-ray very soon.' She's a nurse; things are looking up. What happened to the humourless paramedic guy?

Wincing through my partially opened and probably fluttering eyelids, I look up as I am wheeled along a corridor with lights above me. Now they're there, now they're not. Like the carpet in the Shining; brrrr, silence, brrrr, silence. The hanging signs pass in an infuriating blur. They aren't designed to be read from flat on your back. My head hurts like a son-of-a-bitch, by the way.

The babying talk continues as I get my head fried. Click, click, click. 'Roll onto your right side.' Click,

click, click. 'Other side now.' You get the idea. Luckily for me I am on my side as I throw up. A quick splurge that splatters almost musically on the tiled floor. The blast radius will be spectacular I expect. I'm not proud; I just don't give a shit. I lie back for a moment and we are off again. Marvellous.

Dr Parker is worried about my x-rays and my blood pressure. 'Yours would be high too mate, if you had been fighting a demon this evening.' I want to point out. I don't but I want to. Would get me sectioned I expect.

'You'll have to stay for observation Father Steel. I will see you again in the morning.' He flaps shut my folder with a finality that will brook no disagreement.

'Fine.' I try not to sound grumpy but fail miserably. Moments later he's gone, white coat flapping behind him like superman. I notice a clock above a door as I am wheeled away. Three eighteen. FFS how much did I miss?

I have missed breakfast, or rather, it sits on my table but the lumpy, now solid, porridge has had it. Why did I ask for porridge? No idea but I did. Anyway I am not forcing that down. This comfy bed is trying to seduce me to sleep again and it has almost won when my room door opens. These are private rooms but this means anyone can walk in, apparently. This anyone is the Bishop. He can come in, I suppose.

'Andrew, how are you feeling?' He's worried about me, I can tell by his face not being in the usual disapproving pose. I try to scoot up but it is too much effort and my head is threatening to explode so I don't bother.

'Not great.' See, I can be civil. He sits on the plastic chair, scraping it closer across the floor. Thanks for that, the sound thunders through my head. His florid, bishoppy, face is too close and out of focus. Probably a good thing all things considered.

'What happened, Andrew?' He is talking quietly which I appreciate more than his usual booming tones. He is in discrete mode. Walls have ears and all that.

'I found the hiding place and we got jumped in the dark by the demon.' Succinct eh?

'I see. Why was Peter with you?' Surprisingly little recrimination in his voice, it appears he just wants answers.

'It's his patch and he had felt it already. He was sensitive enough to not go in alone.' I really can't be arsed. I am going to get a telling off and no doubt I will behave like a teenager. I know I am meant to tell very few people about what I do but I didn't tell Peter until after his up close and personal encounter. He would have worked it out anyway, he isn't stupid.

'That was foolhardy. Why didn't you get the police first?' Disapproval fills every word as they reach my ears. Here comes the telling off. Will I ever recover? I expect so.

'I didn't actually expect it to be in there. I was following its trail from the new crime scene.' At least I had something to report. Not exactly progress but a semblance of something that could lead to progress.

'At least we know what the human form looks like.' Silver lining and all that.

'It has been on the news.' The Bishop doesn't seem impressed by my version of progress. He waits. It must be my turn again.

'The Demon,' I begin and see the furrows starting on his forehead 'can take over human bodies. I don't know if they need to be dead first. The one he's in stinks and won't last long.' Best put all my cards on the metaphorical table.

'That should make it easier to narrow down which other-worlder we are dealing with.' His correction is as subtle as a brick. I didn't use the approved term from the lexicon. He can be such a stickler.

'He may have been in a few meat-sacks which might explain why we haven't had much luck finding him.' Meat sacks causes the eyebrows to shoot up and a frown to settle in full force upon his face. Besides I have had enough of this conversation already. Hopefully he will bugger off soon, he didn't bring any grapes or flowers.

'Andrew,' There is a warning of displeasure under the tone 'Why is it here?' This is the crucial question. A question, to which, I have no answer. There must be a reason; psychopathic murdering demons don't just appear on their own. I hope.

'Someone summoned it? An escapee from some prophecy? I don't know.' Not the answer he is looking for.

'I have people looking into The Writings but nothing yet. We will keep looking but we need some sort of direction.' He is trying to help, bless him.

'I will go back to all the scenes and see what I can glean. Besides, now I have been up close and personal, I might be better placed to make progress.' Of course, I need the Doc to let me out.

Morning it seems is a nebulous term to mean 'whenever I can be bothered'. In this case Doctor Parker meant two in the afternoon. I suppose it is still morning somewhere in the mid-Atlantic. Pissy? Me? You bet your sweet bippy I am. Lunch was pish, too, but at least I ate it. The only saving grace is my nurse; she is fantastic. She has kept an eye on me; fed me Paracetamol and tea and only taken my blood pressure four times. She has a beautiful voice and the clearest, shiny blue eyes anyone has a right to. No wonder they are often called angels. As if on cue, she pops her head around the door.

'Doctor Parker is on his way along the ward. He won't be long.' Her smile is a little ray of sunshine. The Bugger better let me out. I have been reading my own chart and my blood pressure is on the way down.

The entry swoosh, of a man on a mission, and Superdoc is in my room. He is scanning the observation notes and giving a running commentary for himself I think. It is like a pre-flight checklist. His eyes flip over the top of the clipboard.

'How's the head Father?' A question flying from amidst his muttering and luckily I was paying attention.

'Just a dull ache. The Paracetamol helps.' No

messing about, I just want to hear a few magic words.

'Well your blood pressure has gone down to safer levels. However you need to see your GP and have it sorted out. It is too high to be healthy in a man your age.' Cheeky Bastard. 'You don't have a cracked skull. You were very lucky. You weren't concussed either which I find remarkable. Don't push your luck too often though.' He is trying to be helpful, I think. 'I would normally keep you for another night but I need your bed and I think you'll be fine. Is there someone who can keep an eye on you?' Yippee freedom is looming on the horizon.

'I live in the seminary. There are plenty of Brothers to look after me.' I try not to do a little happy dance.

'Good then, Father, you can go home and rest for a couple of days. GP for the blood pressure and take care of yourself. You aren't as young as you once were.' He is scribbling on my notes.

'Thank you Doctor Parker.' I say but feel an near overwhelming urge to tell him to fuck off. He has all the bedside manner of a pathologist. Still, I will be out of here and that is all that matters.

Chapter 7

After two days of molly-codling I have definitely had enough. The Bishop has been putting a few words out. Obviously of the 'look after Andrew' type because my room might as well have been fitted with a revolving door. The stream of visitors has been well orchestrated and unending. The fact that no one has brought a dram with them suggests a level of organisation that doesn't usually exist in the seminary. Even Father Ignatius (if ever a candidate for changing your name by deed poll existed) didn't bring me his hip flask of dubious whisky, which normally I'd refuse. It has led to many a black out and hangover from hell.

My headache has, all but, gone and I am able to move about without feeling that my head will explode. Apparently there has been a breakthrough in our case. I say our but DI White has been most inattentive since my brush with chummy. No Calls, no flowers, not get well soon card. Nada. Zip. Hee-Haw. Almost like a one night stand with a promise to call. That was until this morning.

The body of our smelly, decaying suspect has turned up at Cockenzie Power Station. He was clogging up an inlet valve or some such. DI White reckons he went in near the River Esk at Musselburgh. Tides or something like that. Anyway, I am up and dressed and raring to go. There is a car on its way. I am only a little bit moist and my shirt is helpfully mopping up the sweat that is leaking from my back pores.

As if by magic, like a taxi booked in advance, my fluorescent panelled cop car arrives to whisk me away to view gruesome remains. I am off to the morgue where, I hope, I have a better time than I did last time. I am sure the morgue technician will feel the same way.

By the time I am deposited at the Edinburgh body store, I feel like a criminal. Sitting in the back of a cop car with two silent cops up front will do that to you, you know, the silent treatment. I wasn't my usual chatty self. Yeah right. It takes a certain type to be a traffic cop and I have had a few run ins with their colleagues in other areas. My balls ache with an old memory. They are the raw materials for the SturmAbteilung.

So it is just me, DI White and the body. A private

viewing of sorts. DI White doesn't want any further questions about my performance. 'It isn't pretty Father.' He pulls open the horizontal fridge. The clunk of the handle and smooth hum as the tray runs out on well lubed acrylic rollers the overture music to our visit. The functional, sterile environment of tiles and the smell of bleach masking the worst of the odd smells that waft out towards me.

DI white unzips the body bag. It is a real treat. The hard plastic teeth pulling apart to reveal a horror reel highlight. It's like a kinder surprise but no chocolate and definitely no toy. The first wave to hit is the stench. The rot has set in and it isn't recent. Then again I already knew that. Eyes have been removed by an ophthalmic seagull and other bits have been nibbled here and there by other denizens of the sea.

I hesitate, letting the psychic banquet wash towards me. Ordinarily I have to touch but this one is almost radioactive. I can see the aura, riven through with cords of black, and it is seeping towards me. Our demon friend has left his mark all over this one.

'Buckle up Buttercup.' I mutter to myself as I reach out to touch a hand that the last time I saw it was wrapped around a clergyman's throat. An instant stabbing sensation travels up my arm causing me to cry out like a big Jessie. I grit my teeth and hope they don't crack under the pressure. As he was already dead, I don't expect to relive his last moments. I get a set of highlights. A series of meaningless images fluttering like a swarm of butterflies – all very colourful and distracting – but very little to explain why him and how his life of drudgery had brought him to this place. I sigh as I let go of the hand. The stabbing pain is turned off like a switch but a cold dull ache remains in its place.

'Anything Father?' DI White is hopeful or expectant; I am not sure which.

'Not really.' I shake my head slowly 'But I will need a few minutes to pray for his immortal soul.' This one needs cleansed and any residual darkness washed away before it is buried in the ground. If not it can mess with the sanctity of the graveyard.

DI White bows his head, bless his little cotton socks. Maybe I should have said 'You need to piss off while I perform some magic shit'. I wait and eventually he gets it. Rather sheepishly he offers to get coffee. See, he is a good guy.

'In the name of the Father, Son and Holy Spirit.' I

mark his forehead with the sign of the cross. The skin feels warm to me. It should be clammy and cold but it isn't. I touch my crucifix to the fleshy forehead and begin to start the Rite of Cleansing. I need to remove the darkness that infested this corpse. All at once the lattice of lines become visible like old Indian ink tattoos. The air around me begins to thrum like a singing bowl.

Torn, sunken eyelids flash open revealing sightless empty sockets. The fingers, all bent and broken, begin to twitch. The hold of the Dark is great on this one. The tattered lips begin to move revealing the ruin of teeth standing on blackened gums. I continue the prayer of cleansing, my crucifix firmly pressed to the skin.

'The power of Christ compels you to leave this faithful servant.' I, all but, shout as the body tries to roll over. It shudders at my command but it doesn't stop. The twitching, spasmodic hands have gripped the sidebars and are now giving leverage. The sizzling on the forehead is loud filling the near silence. Heat builds up on my hand as the darkness fights against my power.

'I command you, in the name of The Father, The

Son and The Holy Spirit.' I practically yell at it. Him. It seems to have raised the cavalry. Footsteps are approaching at the gallop, that's all I need, witnesses.

A dark fugue is seeping from it, I am not calling it a zombie, eye sockets, mouth, nose. Running down it's face like exhaled smoke; just not in rings. The burning on its forehead is causing pain but it isn't enough to stop it. With its hands on the bars it pushes up and away from my glowing crucifix. A voice filled with pain slips words from a mouth that should no longer speak.

DI White crashes into the room, and almost comically slides to a halt beside me. This is not what he expected, I can assure you. 'Oh my God. Fuck.' Not four words I would chose as my last but perhaps I'm just fussy. DI White's mouth is opening and closing but nothing else is being produced. Our, not quite, peacefully dead friend manages to force out almost intelligible words.

'The Master is coming. The Master is coming. Death. Death.' Sounds that fill us with dread.

'Be Afraid. Be very afraid.' Is what is charging through my mind. DI White is staring, poor chap. There is no training for this in his handbooks.

The mouth opens super wide and a fountain of

deep black-red blood flies through the air towards us.

Hitting like a water cannon, it drives us back. Gallons of it; more than could ever be in a human body fly through the air. The morgue is splattered and covered in a cone of deep crimson.

The body collapses with a soft, squishy thud back onto its trolley. Thank God, which I do. The attendant has just opened the door behind us; he missed the show I hope. DI White is still rooted to the spot. The stench is horrendous and the vomiting starts behind me. Wimps.

Chapter 8

The Bishop's residence is very grand. Even more so if you get the full effect by walking up the gravel drive. Ordinarily I park my, less than new, red Nissan Sunny beside the sleek black Volvo but today I got the bus. After all with roads all churned up to put in the trams, driving in the capitol is so not a pleasure. Anyway, the solid stone seventeenth century manor house is a beautiful building. It is a hefty Episcopal statement about the permanence and importance of the church. Size, as they never say, matters in far too many things. Compensating much?

I ring the bell, set into a stone circle not a poxy plastic thing, and wait. I have been summoned, asked for lunch but what's the difference. The Bishop wants an update and that might not take long. I wait expectantly for the door to respond immediately and it doesn't. It gives me time to buff my shoes on my calves to get a wee shine. I am just finished when the dog-collared-butler opens the door.

'Good Afternoon Father Andrew, you are to go on

through to the study.' So polite, it makes my teeth ache. No disapproving frown to set off my shoulder chip; so I need to behave. Removing my coat, I smile as I hand it to him. 'Thank you.' He isn't impressed at being treated like the help. I know I am being a bit petty but old habits die hard.

Anyway, the study is a veritable Aladdin's cave of very old and interesting books. The mahogany ocean-going desk sits in front of the French windows but nowhere is the bishop to be found. I should probably just sit on the chesterfield and wait but I love to peruse books. Too many haven't moved in years but the dust is removed regularly by the house elves. My eye stops on one I haven't seen or read before. 'The Dominion of the Earthbound.' It looks old. Old enough to be serious and it is bound in light coloured leather. The lettering is black, which is what caught my eye. I sneak a peek at it; lifting it quickly before I get caught. Hand in the cookie jar as it were.

It is heavier than it looks, a satisfying heft and definitely a reading table book; not an in-bedder. The opening page is a lithographic print of the Great Casting Out of Satan and his gang from heaven. It is much stylised but beautifully done. On the next page the author of this tome is announced. No idea who he is but I am sure I should know. A flick of the very expensive paper pages and we are off on an illicit journey.

'The Kingdom of Heaven was purged of the followers of Lucifer and following their casting out, over the earth they gained dominion.' A gloomy start, if ever there was one.

'Andrew.' The boom of Bishop Michael's voice fills the study and I jump slamming the book shut. Looking round I try not to look guilty, fat chance of that. I fail miserably. 'How are you feeling?' He is crossing the carpet and can see the book in my hands. I hand it to him as he nears, contraband surrendered. He almost doesn't frown at my invasion of his things. The Dominion of the Earthbound is safely tucked back on the shelf. It will remain an unscratched intellectual itch for me until I get another itch somewhere else.

'Come, sit.' His hand waves like a traffic controller. He seems to be in a reasonable mood, although I am sure I can change that. The banalities pass without a hitch and he presses the 'go' button.

'How's the case coming along?' It is the give me an update demand.

'Slowly.' It's best not to overstate progress that doesn't actually exist. I wait a moment and I suppose it is still my turn. 'I had an event at the morgue yesterday that gives me concerns.' This is a new ploy for me, it's like asking for help I actually need.

'How so?' The vertical line that splits his forehead deepens a little but not the full on disapproval face yet.

'The body our demon friend has been wearing got up and spoke before showering me with blood.' I might need to provide some details but these can wait. Bishop Michael's eyebrows have shot up and are hiding under his hairline.

'Dear Lord.' His eyes raise heavenward. I manage not to smirk. 'What did it say?' He wants the details then.

"The Master is Coming!' a couple of times.' I pause and add casually 'And death a few times, too.' I manage to keep my face straight, now is not really the time for humour.

'That sounds ominous. Have you spoken to anyone about this yet?' I shake my head; no chance. His eyes are a wee bit shiny, he wants the gory details.

'The blood fountain covered DI White and myself;

missed the morgue tech though.' More witnesses to give the Bishop nightmares.

'Oh Andrew this is getting out of hand.' A public relations disaster is looming, obviously. DI White and I will say nothing and the morgue tech knows nothing; so all will be fine. I have been wrong before, though. I can see a lengthy call to the Home Office for Bishop Michael this afternoon. A trouble shared is a trouble doubled I think.

There is a pregnant (though I'd call it lengthy) pause which looks like stretching on for eternity. It is interrupted by the tea-bearer bringing in the tray. The frown upon his master's brow gives him pause. Is it for the interruption? He'll never know. At least there is a plate of Hobnobs; not chocolate ones but still Hobnobs. Wordlessly he removes himself.

'Is there a pattern emerging? I hear that DI White is highly thought of.' The Bishop has his thinking cap on; and you thought it was a Mitre. I have a mouthful of biscuit so he will have to muse a bit longer. I try to crunch quietly. Perhaps I should pour the tea and be mother.

'No pattern I can see as yet.' I manage to speak without spraying crumbs everywhere. A slurp of tea washes away any issue of full-biscuit-mouth, I can speak again.

'I don't like this one Andrew.' He is looking out the French windows. I make a face as it's obviously my fault. I hope he can't see my reflection in the glass.

'Neither do I. The bodies are dumped so I haven't discovered if where they died is significant. I will walk his trail again today. That might turn something up.' I swig my tea not letting it get cold.

'There's a ritual element to this Andrew. What for and for whom we may not find out but it is there. Do we need Father Jeremy's help? He is still in the Capitol.'

'It couldn't hurt.' I say out loud. My inner dialogue is more of the For Fucks Sake variety.

'I'll give him your number and let you sort it out. I have meetings in London for the rest of the week. Hopefully, between you, it will be resolved by my return.' He picks up his cup, doesn't skip a beat as he swallows the very cool tea. Was that a deadline? Sounded very much like it to me. I'd better get lost then. Sent out to find a demon and discover its nefarious plot. Stop the plot and avert any disaster by next Monday before the Bishop parks his arse back in that seat.

    I can feel my face souring up as I am effectively dismissed. Happy bunny I, most definitely, am not. I take a handful of hobnobs; an act of rebellion that is probably a better idea than 'Fuck off!' No sign of lunch either.

Chapter 9

Edinburgh is a lovely place, full of culture, architecture and arseholes. Well, at least, this bit is. The Gardens, all resplendent and colourful being enjoyed by families and tourists, is the scene of a yob-a-thon. A host, nay a plague, of football-top-wearing-post-pubescent idiots is romping along making a racket. Their mono-syllabic, high brow, chants are such a great advert for a cultural hub like the capitol.

I manage to tutt loudly and shake my head; complaining in the true Scottish style. Say nothing, do nothing, moan later to anyone who'll listen. Oh dear they have spotted the dog-collar. The finger pointing and childish shoving of each other has begun. If only this could be an original effort I might be less irritated by them and their nonsense.

'Paedo, Paedo, Paedo-phile.' They chant in unison. It is like a hive-mind with a brain cell between them. They march off with their new tune; all gleeful and pleased with themselves. Their lusty and enthusiastic noise would shame many a choir in the church for volume but that is about as positive as I can get. I'm not sure if these are home-grown or imported eejits as they all look the same to me. Knuckle draggers of the lowest order and thankfully receding into the distance.

The peaceful reflection I had been enjoying is well and truly shattered leaving me grumpier than usual and my latte has long since disappeared leaving a foamy, lumpy dreg in the bottom of the recyclable cup. The FFS face is definitely on display to the outside world, a great advert for a caring clergy. After a sigh that has its roots in the soles of my shoes I decide to visit the National Gallery of Scotland, a wonderful place. I go, not for the paintings, but for a decent cup of coffee and the most delicious Viennese whirls. Besides, it isn't that warm out here anyway.

Sitting in the corner giving off the 'don't bother me vibe', coffee and cake before me, I am irked that someone feels it is okay to park themselves in the seat opposite. A corpulent fellow with a belly that practically shelves over the top of his trousers makes me feel less depressed at my keg belly.

'Is this taken?' But his arse is descending as he

asks. A presumptive possession of the limited real estate if ever there was one. I presume I have to answer with something less sarcastic that I want to.

'No. Go ahead.' I manage politely, my inner sarcasm kept well in check this time. 'Too bloody late if it is.' I really want to say as I pull out my phone. I am feigning a busyness that doesn't exist while my peace is shattered by my slurping companion. If people growled then we might avoid these situations.

My phone buzzes and squeaks causing me to drop it on the table with a clatter, a text arriving as I pretended to be busy. That'll teach me. I manage to not exclaim my surprise with an expletive but only just. Father Jeremy, apparently, has sent me a text. I look ruefully up at my table sharer. He has a wee grin on his face and I try to prevent a sour look appearing on mine. It seems that Jezza wants to meet now. I suggest we meet at the foot of the Scott Monument and a few buzzes later, it is a date. I am not bloody going up it though.

It is not warm and the slightest wind seems to steal all the heat out of the day. I see Jeremy moving along with the flow of humanity, just one more face in a sea. Unfortunately he has seen me too, and now he is waving like an idiot. Not a discrete hand up, here I am. No, it is more a Donkey from Shrek waving about like a demented ecstatic. A village somewhere has lost its idiot.

'I see you, you arse.' I mutter to myself as I wave back, once. I have definitely descended into middle-aged grumpy man. Still, Father Jeremy ought to be a help and Lord knows I need it.

'Andrew!' He is almost breathy in his excitement or perhaps it is the exertion. His cheeks are flushed just below his little glasses, almost cherubic looking, and he looks so neat and tidy. We must be playing opposites; neat priest and crumpled priest. Oh well.

'Father Jeremy, lovely to see you.' I manage to fake enthusiasm. Our handshake is brief and functional. I stuff my hands back in my pockets, too cold for no gloves.

'Shall we get a coffee? I have much to share that might be useful.' Good old Jezza, overstating his usefulness before we start. I wonder what dusty, crusty old scholar can tell me what is going on. Still the offer of a coffee is never a bad thing; for some folks it is a pint but coffee is a good second choice. I am on a hat-trick of lattes and will probably get a little hyper; might need to be a decaf.

'Sounds good, let's go to Jenners. It's just over there.' I offer like a proper host, after all Jeremy is a visitor to our fair city. Jenners is a beautiful old-fashioned department store for the well to-do. The building is gorgeous and the price tags are remarkably reasonable. They do a lovely cream tea in their café on the fifth floor, too.

I love the inner stairwell, all open to each floor, and the railings of carved wood and iron decoration. Opulence delivered from another time making it feel just a little bit special. They even have a bra fitting department, not that I have availed myself of that service personally.

In no time at all we have passed the clouds of expensive perfumes and ascended (using the lift) to the refreshments. The soft lounge seats in the corner are discrete enough, I hope. I have barely stirred my Americano (the latte was unavailable) when Father Jeremy begins.

'It's a ritual. Or at least there has been one.' That explains everything, obviously. I don't interrupt as I have an urge to sarcasm bomb him.

'The other-worlder has only 28 days to complete its task, whatever it is. It has one lunar cycle to be exact.' His glasses have slipped a little and he's peering over them like a mad professor. Maybe I am meant to be more appreciative of this kernel of information. A mini pause has begun but I crumble to avoid a comment to regret.

'Okay.' I manage to say without giving myself away.

'We need to know when the first killing took place. That will tell us when the time runs out.' He looks at me expectantly and I am caught on the hop.

'I don't know exactly when the first killing took place.' Best be upfront about my deficiencies. 'But it was found on the third. So no more than a day or two before that I expect.' I can ask DI white for details and pull out my phone to text.

'That doesn't leave very long. Whatever is going on will come to a climax on Sunday. Five more days.' Jeremy helpfully reminding me it is Tuesday. I don't snigger at his climax although the image almost twitches my lips.

'How many killings will there be?' Maybe there will be some good news. I doubt it but one can hope.

'It depends.' He begins and then slurps his chocolate. A grown man drinking hot chocolate with pink and white mini-marshmallows, I was almost embarrassed for him when he ordered it. 'There may be four for cardinal points or five if it is a pentagram.' The little mallow residue on his upper lip is distracting.

'So one or two more then?' I know we have three already. If there has been another one during my convalescence then the Master may already be on his way.

'The last one must take place on the final day of the lunar cycle, probably under moonlight.' At least that is useful to know.

'Is there a manual somewhere I've missed?' Sorry, it slipped out. It's probably called Summoning for Dummies, I can see the yellow and black cover right now.

'Not exactly, Andrew.' He smiles and slurps. 'I have gleaned these from the archives over the years. The details are scattered across texts and witness accounts. Some are very old.' Smugness fills his voice and face. I want to growl again.

'Any clues as to where it will happen?' I'll bet your tomes don't tell you that Jezza.

'Not really. However, it will be somewhere within the confines of the summoning perimeter.' He is winging it, I can tell, as he is waving his cup about in a vague airy gesture. Never play poker Jeremy the bad boys will steal your pocket money.

'So Edinburgh then?' Thanks a fucking bunch.

'It needs to be on holy ground, too.' Jeremy adds to the mix. And the hits they keep on coming. I wonder what else he will omit to mention. No doubt I will find out when it is most critical

'Edinburgh, church, Sunday night under moonlight.' I smile but want to scream. 'He's as good as caught.' Jeremy is serious, for fucks sake. And he's on my side; with help like this who needs hindrance. My Americano is finished too. I look at the empty cup and sigh.

Chapter 10

I suppose I should be thankful; after all it confirms what I suspected. The killings have been taking place elsewhere and the bodies dumped. Well, apart from the last one, I know it happened in the alley. Small wonder the pattern won't fit and the cops have no idea how to fit them together. It is the same killer though. That's something at least of which I am certain.

Plan of action is to find the actual sites and plot them on a map of Edinburgh. That way I can find the point where it will culminate on Sunday night. Thwart the demon plot and kill the baddie. Simples as the little meerkat on the telly would say. DI White will be so impressed. I am not surprised that every case seems to end in a complete disaster and an extended stay in an NHS bed.

Edinburgh is a great place. No really, it is. However, it is old. Old towns and cities have lots of one thing, churches. It was the hobby of choice for centuries for the wealthy when times were boring build a chapel, if it got really dull build a big church or a Cathedral. They are lovely and the tourists flock round the bigger ones clicking their cameras. For me though, the truly vast list of churches, cemeteries and possible sites is a real pain. Add to this the list of 'newer' religions and my list is getting longer and longer a bit like Santa's naughty list.

I need a bigger map. So far mine looks like a massive spot the ball with lots (and lots) of little crosses on it. I wonder if the police have a decent map they would let me deface? Looking back at my handiwork (an hour or so of effort) and I conclude that it tells me nothing. I need to find the first site and go from there. That might just be the key to finding the others. A needle in a haystack springs to mind.

'DI White.' He sounds tired to me, poor sod.

'Steel here. I need a map, a big one of the city, if you have such a thing.' Probably should have done the small talk thing. Oh well, too late now. This playing nicely is such hard work.

'No problem, what are you thinking?' DI White is such a helpful fellow and he never seems to be too upset at my demands.

'Churches are the key to this. The murders are taking place in churches or church grounds. It's part of a ritual.' I might as well give him the full picture. It will save time later. Of course, that's about all I have to contribute.

'There are lots of churches, synagogues and mosques in the city. It will be a big list.' No shit Sherlock.

'We can start with the ones near where the girls were dumped. He can't have carried them too far.' I attempt to minimise the size of the task at hand.

'OK. Come on down and we can look at it.' He sounds resigned to a long day. He doesn't know the half of it.

'Oh White,' I catch him before he hangs up 'we are missing a couple of bodies. There will be four or five culminating with a last one on Sunday night.' Bombshell dropped and bomber heading for home. I can feel his grip on the receiver tightening.

'Dear God.' He whispers. I can almost picture a head in hands moment.

'Exactly and the last one was a recreational kill; not part of the pattern at all.' I like to share good news early and often.

'We need help. The Brass are going to be so pleased to hear this.' There's an accompanying rustle of papers coming from his end.

'I'll be there as soon as I can.' I hope he finds that comforting.

'Finding the bodies is not important just now.' Direct but true, so I keep trampling on. 'The sites of the murders will help us stop the last one on Sunday night.' Spelling things out to rather pedestrian thinking plods seems to be my Sisyphean task.

'Yes, Father, but the bodies will hold vital clues.' Chief Superintendent Nitwit wants a body search for an unspecified number of corpses and in unspecified areas.

'Like the ones we have in the morgue?' I lob my grenade into his argument. He gives me a look. I get it a lot; it's a cross between 'Fuck off' and 'you are disrespecting me.' I might be immune to it though. Chief Stupid-intendent Cousins gives a little mini-sigh and capitulates. I can always play my 'I am in charge' card but I save that for emergencies.

'All right Father, I take your point. How do you think we should proceed?'

'We need to check as many churches and their grounds for blood splatters. If we identify a possible site then DI White and I can check it out and see what it tells us.' Just a simple, little task obviously.

'That's a lot of churches.' Cousins doesn't look happy but that's life. I wonder if this is what the Bishop calls playing nice? Probably not.

'Sooner we start, the sooner we will get a lead.' I try to be upbeat; there's only so much he can take in one go. I could have said 'Let's turn that frown upside down' but I didn't.

DI White hands me a coffee in a proper cup too. It even looks the right colour; the coffee not the mug. PC Jill is bringing one for the chief Super. A packet of Hobnobs appears as if by magic. Cousins is a biscuit man; a double dunker and his deftness at consuming the oaty-goodness of Hobnobs is a well honed skill. A few biscuits in and he speaks, his face and tone much friendlier.

'We have ten uniformed officers available now and we will be able to pull in some traffic guys later this afternoon. That will make a start.' He's thinking out loud and I let him continue as I stuff my face.

The frown on DI white's face is getting deeper. He is thinking, I hope. 'It'll still take days we don't have sir.'

'We don't have any more juice to do it, I'm afraid.' Cousins is scanning for more of the disappearing biscuits.

'What if we ask the Clergy to do it? We could get each of them to check their grounds and church buildings. Might give us a start?' I hear myself uttering such helpful suggestions and am surprised. No hint of sarcasm tainting them either.

'Let's get on with it then.' Cousins has decided in his evaporating-post-biscuit-glow. To hear is to obey, said no one ever.

What do clergymen and women do on a midweek morning? I have no idea but not many of them are answering their phones. I might be on a few blocked lists but I doubt I am on them all. PC Jill is having the same sort of luck but at least she has managed to contact a few. I swig my cup of tea-substance and find it all but empty. My face is a mirror of my inner unhappiness and frustration and I plop it down a little more firmly than I really meant. Another voicemail box. I manage to articulate a message and leave the contact number.

'Dear Father Campbell there is a demon running

amok in town. Please check your church and grounds for blood splatters as it may have been the site of a satanic summoning.' Is screaming around in my head and, I hope, not the words I actually say aloud.

Next on the list is the attractive sounding 'Light of the World Church of the Lord.' I snort in derision, I am such a snob. No bugger in there either. I put the receiver back and decide to make the tea. PC Jill has at least got someone to talk to.

I waggle my mug and mouth the 'Tea?' question. Her bobbing ponytail confirms the yes. It'll be the first useful thing I've done in the last hour. DI White waggles his too; my promotion to tea-boy has been made official. Years of study to end up making the tea; I have peaked, obviously.

DI White and I are the flying squad. As soon as we get a possible we are going to swoop down upon the site with all sirens blaring and lights flashing. The Sweeney would be so proud; I am Reagan and get to shout a lot.

Uniformed officers have been sent to the closest possible sites (based on where the bodies were found) but we have heard nothing yet. How hard can this be? I thought we had cracked it with my genius suggestion but apparently not. We have some traffic cops to use this afternoon. I hope they have been briefed properly as the list of churches and suchlike is a long one and we aren't there yet.

My efforts at tea may prevent me being given the task ever again. The tea looked fine at the kettle but is probably a bit on the strong – undrinkable side. Better that than the milk with a hint of tea in it. It is hot and wet so it will have to do.

Next on my list is 'Magdalene Chapel, Morningside', it sounds delightful. It is ringing and I have just burned my tongue on the tea. A silent bout of swearing ensues, fuck-fuckitty-fuck.

'Good morning, Father Andrew, how can I help you?' How on earth did he know it was me, I nearly laugh.

'Good morning, I am calling on behalf of Edinburgh Police. We need your help.' I pause, gives him time to say 'of course' or something like that.

'We need you to check your church and grounds for anything out of the ordinary. We are particularly looking for blood splatters.' I pause again.

'My Goodness.' He sounds camper than a row of tents. The shocked tone tells me he might need some assistance.

'This is a murder enquiry and you need to check as soon as possible and confirm back to the task force here.' Better get him to do it before he needs a wee lie down.

'Oh my,' He splutters 'of course, I will. Right away.' He'll be running about like a wet hen and will probably faint if he finds blood.

'Thank you. As soon as possible, if you please.' Get off the phone and move on. How people manage to work in call centres I don't know. Nobody answers their phone and when they do they are unhelpful. I have been doing this for ninety three minutes and I have had enough already. Chapeau to those who have to do this all day every day.

Chapter 11

'We have a hit.' DI White calls over to me. I am under whelmed. I was expecting a ghost-busters-esque lights flashing and siren. Oh well. I didn't get a pony for Christmas either.

It seems Father Andrew at Magdalene Chapel has found something, so forgive me if I am sceptical. I'm betting this is a false alarm. He was such a drama queen on the phone he would be desperate to take part in the enquiry. It would give him something to gossip to parishioners about; how he helped solve the murders. I can feel my face looking sour.

Traffic in the Capitol is really just an exercise in clutch control. Movement is sluggish like, I imagine, the turgid Mississippi river. Moving through the traffic like a big catfish, slow, slow then zip through a gap to the next bottleneck. Luckily for us DI White is a catfish and hasn't used his lights yet. I would be sirens and lights by now but there are rules I believe. Who knew?

'Won't be long now.' DI White states it like a fact.

He has said that very same thing four times now. His credibility has taken a knock.

'No worries.' I manage to be civil but my sour puss is looking out; so hopefully he will believe me. I want to scream 'Use the fucking siren!' but I'll keep that in for the next nearly-there-a–gram

It turns out that not long was less than a minute as a beautiful little Gothic chapel heaves into view. A well tended gravel car park welcomes us with a reassuring crunch. Like Crockett and Tubbs we dismount the car. Wish I had my shades on; we are so cool.

I can feel the power of God through my feet. This chapel is very pure. It isn't often I can feel it outside. The sun is playing across the stained glass, showing their craftsmanship to any who care to look. The tableau of Mary on one side and Saint Michael on the other is an odd mix. My frown, as I can't put my finger on it, gives away my grumpiness. They are very lifelike, not stylised representations, and that is even more unusual. Curiouser and curiouser, as Alice might say.

The Oak studded door with black iron hinges shout that this door will keep all comers out. For a heartbeat

White and I look at it then both go at once for the iron ring handle. I let him do it, a little push and the house of God is open.

I am getting goosebumps as I cross the threshold, not creepy ones, good ones. It's like the loving caress of a recharge as I feel the tingles run through me. I try not to purr as we move into the church and avail myself of the holy water in the silver font. I genuflect and cross myself as we turn to face the high altar. The dark stained wooden pews are dust free and have seen many a pious buttock. This is a Holy island in a sea of amorality. I will keep this stored away for future emergencies, one never knows when a real emergency may present itself. Lucky is the Priest with this charge.

As if on cue here he comes, practically mincing, towards us. I school my face trying for bland. Hopefully it doesn't just show sour. What is it with the camp prancing? Buggered if I know.

'Father Andrew? DI White.' Cop takes charge, I nod not trusting myself yet.

'There's some blood behind the church, in the graveyard. It is just terrible.' No prelims just a near hysterical panic and the only thing missing is the flapping hands.

'Take us there, please Father. Time is of the essence.' See, I can be polite. A firm hand is usually what is needed with the highly strung in the priesthood. I can do firm.

It is like a switch. Halfway down the tidy graveyard pea-gravel path the Holy switch goes off. Holy – not holy. Consecrated – not consecrated. The back of the graveyard isn't part of the church. There must have been some enlargement that was never consecrated, probably part of the various local government reorganisations where land often changed hands. I'll bet no one thought about ensuring the ground was claimed and consecrated. This might be the place after all. The boundary wall of the church is a good twenty feet further on. There are no yew trees for the Unforgiven to be buried beneath.

'Over there.' Father Andrew points a shaky looking finger. Does he manicure them? 'Near the Angel at the back.' He stands rooted to the spot, obviously not wishing to get any closer.

'Thanks. We'll take it from here.' I try to sound sincere but his uber-campness is really irritating. DI White has moved on, not waiting.

In an accidental pincer, we surround the angel looking over the dearly departed resting place of Alexander Lothian and his clan. Going by the list and dates, this is a family plot. The Angel is a thing of beauty. Well sculpted and very smooth; a very expensive piece. It has withstood the determined efforts of Mother Nature and Father Time. I want to run my fingers along the surface but remember we have an audience.

'There's blood all right.' DI White is snapping on his gloves as he scans around for a source. I might have missed the large pool and splash of blood bright in the daylight or perhaps I would not have spotted the lovely spray up the back of the plinth being blind and all. It isn't new blood, I can tell that by looking. It isn't that old either.

'There's more here.' DI White is moving to the wall. I suppose I should go look but it is just more blood. If it is our guy why didn't anyone hear anything? There are houses not that far away. There isn't that much cover either; the graveyard isn't polluted with trees like many are. This one is open to the sky on this side. There could be some cover from the larger monuments and crypts, I suppose.

A grim look has settled on DI White's usually professional cop face. He stands with his hand on his radio thing.

'The trail leads to the wall and over. Is it our guy?' He looks expectantly.

I am caught a little off guard; I was looking at the headstones nearby. Dawdling, you might say. 'What? Oh right. I will know in a moment.' I am so not looking forward to doing this. Father Andrew is standing on the path as far away as he can be but still claim to be taking part. Obviously, I was too subtle with my 'piss off' earlier. He looks like the last kid to get picked at the football. He is so uncomfortable being near to a crime scene. I'd best go behind the Angel and out of sight. I wouldn't want him to faint after all.

I'm not squeamish, at least not any more. Today, however, I am reluctant and I am not sure why. I wonder if it is because I know what I might experience. Evisceration of the victims has been horrible and once seen is there for permanent recall at random times and places. I take the deepest breath I can before I let my hand slip across the blood on the plinth steps at the back.

I almost smile as I get a pleasant surprise. No jolt

of pain and savage re-living the event. She is walking hand in hand with it. The Demon has her within its thrall. I don't recognise her from our incident boards. This is a new one waiting to be found elsewhere. We are further behind than we knew. She feels calm, the skinned knees and grazed shins from the climb over the wall are ignored. I can feel them even though she didn't.

I hope she took a good look round before he kills her. The actual site may hold evidence for DI White, whatever he can make of it. I feel sudden sharp stabs into the back of my hand and realise his claws have just extended burying themselves in her soft flesh. A puzzled, foggy moment as she looks down to see his scaly talons submerged in her hand and the red blood running freely over them.

The scream she tries to get out is lost as he clamps a crushing fist around her throat. Very little sound escaped her after this. The hypnosis is gone replaced by a terror that mankind should never have known. I feel my face contorting as hers did, the tears running over my face only this time they aren't thick with Avon mascara. A brain numbing thudding blow echoes through me as her head collides with a nearby gravestone.

Then he took her. Roughly and with a level of rapture that is sickening in its intensity. Luckily she is barely conscious, as his frenzied thrusts take him over the edge. He casts his seed onto the holy ground, attempting to defile the consecration that has lain for centuries. I am unsteady and my gorge is rising I lean against a handily placed chunk of stone.

With barely a post-coital hug the demon carries her behind the angel and guts her. I manage to shut out the act of his talons twisting the intestines and feel only an ache. Her life passes quickly as her blood pulses out. It doesn't take long. 'Mum.' A plaintive last little whimper escapes her lips. It is over.

Like the flapping end from a projector reel, I take a moment to stop trying to watch. There is no more. My eyes open again on the real world and a few blinks clear away the tears that I shed with her.

The ache in my core and the pain in my soul are reminders of why we are here. DI White is looking at me in an odd way. Father Andrew looks a bit horrified and ghoulishly fascinated too.

'You all right?' DI White breaks the moment. He knows something happened but he just has no idea what. He doesn't try to touch me, which I appreciate. It is obvious I am fine, isn't it?

'I need a moment. It is our guy.' I am still leaning on a headstone it's solidity and permanence a godsend. I wipe my nose, which has twin streamers and I realise that I must look a fright. I often forget about the tears, as they come so often. I have a hankie somewhere and the patting of all my pockets until I find it, is a ritual in itself.

I hear White on the airwave (or whatever they call walkie-talkies these days) our find is a new scene and the circus will be on its way. I wonder what her name was. Everyone who is killed leaves a hole somewhere in some other life. Someone will be waiting or looking for her. Someone will miss her voice and smile, I can feel tears building. Do they really need to know she was raped and then slaughtered? Does anyone ever need to hear that?

I look over at Magdalene chapel and feel my anger rising like a tsunami. My grip on the headstone is painful but I need something to hurt. A nail on my index finger splits giving me a pain to cherish. Getting angry at God is like shouting at the sea; utterly pointless. I can feel the heat of my anger like a spike of bile burning in my gut.

'Father Andrew?' DI White approaches, gently, timid almost.

'What?' I snap like a total diva. His face is a picture. I just kicked a puppy or killed Bambi. I just want everyone to fuck off and leave me alone for a minute. Is it too much to expect?

'Father Andrew has put the kettle on. You should take a few.' His kindness is misplaced but appreciated. I would have told me to go 'fuck myself'.

'Sorry. Thanks I will.' I pull my spikes back in and attempt rapprochement. 'She is a new victim. Raped then killed.' And with that joyous news I walk like a man who has shit himself towards the chapel and the reviving tea.

Chapter 12

'It's all about the sex, Jeremy?' I am being patient but I really want to scream down the phone. He's convinced the consecrated ground is the key and I'm not. It might be but the sex is definitely important to this whole thing. We are dealing with one sick Mo-fo of a demon. I can feel the grip on my phone tightening and my jaw clenching as he twitters on.

'I hear what you are saying but can you look into the rituals with sex as part of the buffet. It brought her a long way to rape her; if she wasn't needed awake he would have knocked her out.' I try to point out the obvious but I can feel a 'For Fucks Sake' itching to be added to my comments.

'Thank you. Let me know soon as. Cheers, bye.' I get off the phone before those milling about in the white suits start to pay me any attention. Their onesies with hoods look ridiculous but then again trying to track a raping, murdering demon might seem ridiculous to them so who am I to cast aspersions.

I am standing on the consecrated bit of the church

grounds; it usually helps me to get my equilibrium back. Today, however, not so much. Father Andrew's tea, though sweet and hot, wasn't much of a restorative either. I feel emptied. Like a big spiritual vacuum cleaner has been inserted and sucked me dry. It is a bit like finding yourself running on empty because you missed breakfast and lunch and it is four in the afternoon.

'Fuck.' I let it out. Only in Scotland does one word say everything quite so efficiently. It is the ubiquity of the word that has made it the punctuation of choice all across the central belt. Sentences can often be littered with it; this time it is the summative use.

'Couldn't agree more Father.' White heard me as he approached from my blind side. His face is pretty grey. We are miles behind and the race ends on Sunday night. DI White knows we need a miracle.

'How many more are we missing do you think?' I catch and hold his eye. He looks a little wild around the edges.

'I thought you said there would be four or five?' He isn't accusing but it is there just beneath the surface.

'It's not an exact science but it looks like the worst

of our nightmares may be on its way. Demons like killing. Perhaps this one is just running amok. I hope not but who knows.' I might as well state the obvious. DI White needs to know that we might be in for a larger body count.

'Fuck.' He joins me in the shortest and most effective sentence in the known world. A moment of perfect misunderstanding hangs in the air between us. I need a pee; don't know what he's thinking.

'It's on the news. They're calling him the graveyard slasher.' PC Jill informs us as we return to the incident room. It's like a whirlwind has been through. A new board with our newest discovery and lurid (sorry glossy) pictures and reports cover its surface. The flat screen television on the far wall has rolling news coverage and a reporter from the scene of 'this latest gruesome murder.' A ticker along the foot of the screen stating in big letters 'Murder.' My face twists, I can't help it.

'Thanks for your help, ya bunch of useless bastards.' I growl and plank my arse on a desk. I start a mental countdown 5,4,3 and my phone buzzes in to life. A look at my screen confirms the caller.

Bishop Michael.

'Steel.' Even though I know it's the boss I pretend I don't. It lets me sound all gruff.

'Andrew 'The Graveyard Slasher'? This is a nightmare. Where are you with this?' His deep voice is filled with anxious undertones.

'We have found another site but no body. This one likes the killing.' I pause, letting him absorb the news. 'There could be a whole raft of them out there waiting to be found.' I let the unfolding mess land in his lap.

'So much for Father Jeremy's four or five then?' He seems a bit put out. Luckily it isn't my fault this time.

'That might be a little on the low side.' I am trying to be helpful but that didn't come out right at all. Around me the police officers are all busy so totally ignoring me.

'You need to find it Andrew and bloody quickly too. The Home Secretary's office has been on the phone three times in the last hour.' He sounds exasperated but not angry at me, at least not yet.

'I will do my best Bishop.' I mumble into my phone. I am watching the rolling news coverage and reading the subtitles. They are basically saying they know nothing and that we know nothing either. The square root of nothing would be closer.

'Andrew this needs stopped. Get Jeremy to hurry up and help.' His tone is the one that says just do as you are told. He's obviously forgotten that Father Jeremy is already helping but I won't remind him of that. A scholar will be a real help, obviously.

'Yes Bishop, I have to go.' Best get off the line before he gives me other things to do.

'Keep me posted.' Another non request and he is gone. No take care or see you later. Not like him to be so abrupt. I bring out the best in people.

'This stuff brings out the crazies. So far it is just the serial confessors but it can get out of hand.' DI White informs the team, of which I am one. 'Uniform are taking up the slack with statements and chasing off the idiots. We have more crime scenes than we can cope with and I am bringing in help from Fife and Glasgow. They'll be here in the morning.' A few groans from the gallery, I am not sure if it's the Fife or the Glasgow bit.

'That better be for the soap dodgers.' I mutter

Soto Voce. There is a tension breaking giggle from the guys. Even DI White cracks a smile. The soap dodgers an affectionate term for the Glasgow contingent.

'All right, settle down.' He pauses leaning forward on the lectern 'This will climax at the weekend, I am reliably informed. There is a ritual element to this that concludes on Sunday. Our focus will be on predicting where it is to occur and catch the Bastard in the act.' He has his audience. They are all focussed and ready now. It is more than I would have told them but DI White knows his guys.

'The lang spoons and the soap dodgers will be picking up the slack as we make the collar.' His smile has a hint of the wolf or maybe maniacal would be closer. He pauses for effect 'Well? Why are you all still sitting here? Get on with it.' Mister Motivator in action.

So we have seven scenes and four bodies; including my close encounter in the community centre. One of the bodies is a recreational kill in my opinion but DI White thinks it counts. Jeremy does too, apparently.

I am staring at the city street map with the

highlighted religious establishments, there is no discernible pattern. No ordinal points, no pentagram emerging; no bloody clue. I know it sounds off but if I were trying to hide a pattern it would be carnage with many extras. As well as a few recreational hits. Then again I could be a sociopath or a psychopath or whichever one it is. One thing is certain, we need more data. Data would mean bodies, so I am careful what I wish for. A sigh escapes my lips. I feel old and tired.

'We have a body.' DC MacBride shouts across the room. The effect is instantaneous, with a collective lurch into action. 'Just down the road from the Morningside Church from today.' Spotty, it seems can't recall the church name.

'Father, you are with me. MacBride, make sure the morgue get their ass on this as soon as. I presume uniform are on the scene?' DI White is barking as his overcoat gets pulled on. MacBride is nodding and writing the commands down. It wasn't that difficult to remember.

'Uniform are on their way, two minutes away.' DC MacBride sings out across the room. I am good to go and DI White is two steps ahead of me as the dynamic duo head for the bat mobile. What a strange pair we make; it is like a cop show in action.

Chapter 13

Casually dumped in a, big grey, household waste bin our other-world friend really has no class. Caroline Forbes, identified from her purse helpfully left in her jacket pocket, is our poor soul from Magdalene Chapel. The indignity of her disposal seems extreme, even to me. The uniformed officers standing guard within the tape perimeter seem particularly discomforted by it. White is busy speaking into his radio as I scan the houses around us. No one is forthcoming with anything useful. I can see the steady progress of two officers as they go from each green-painted council door to the next. An exercise in futility but one that needs to be completed and added to the evidence log.

These big omnium bins, with their little roller wheels have revolutionised the handling of domestic waste. Long gone are the days of the bin man carrying the bin out to the scaffy truck; now we put our bins at the kerbside and a few button presses later they are tipped into the compactor wagon. At least the body wasn't tipped inside the truck. It had been left untouched as it was the wrong bin. Today was green bin day; plastic recycling not general waste. The bin men had just rolled on by leaving the gruesome contents undisturbed. The woman from number 29 had gone out to retrieve her bin and looked at the offending wrong bin. She was sitting in the back of the ambulance, having taken a turn.

I am always surprised that people these days are able to walk past anomalies and not feel even a little bit curious about them. Two days that bin had been at the kerbside. Two days that no one noticed the reek. Two days that little red drops on the pavement had been missed or ignored. Two days that no one even peeked inside. Two days of tutting and moaning to spouses about the inconsiderate sod who had put out, and left out, the wrong bin. A disgrace no doubt. Community? It seems to be seeping away under the onslaught of modern life. Hundreds of little personal castles with little connection or care for the castles built in the same row.

'Mum' had been her last thought. Her last word of choice and one that said so much. Somewhere her mum would be receiving the worst news that would ever reach her ears. The cruelty of a random event in the cosmic battle would leave little possible comfort for her maternal soul. A peace that even our victory and justice would never return to her. Forever her heart would be broken, shattered by a cruel fate. A wrong place, wrong time that would never be understood and a 'Why?' would haunt her all the days of her life. I hoped that there were siblings of Caroline Forbes that her mother could hold tight to her breast.

The prickling around my eyes was my own, not a recollection of past horrors. My heartsick sorrow for a woman I have never met who would soon be called on to visit the viewing room and identify a cleaned up yet still ruined body. I let out the breath that was making my chest hurt and looked round the ordinary street. I needed to do something. Anything. The twitch of a curtain revealed a face that held something. It wasn't ghoulish interest; it was terror. My eyes had caught the looker. The witness that had seen something. I marched straight towards the door, there was no point in her not answering.

'I am Father Steel. I am with the police.' I spoke firmly watching her face take in the dog collar and the reference to the police giving me the authority to compel her obedience. Her housecoat was clamped around her like a suit of armour against the world. The flowers a bit faded and worn but not shabby though, her hair that silver grey that old women get rinsed with blues and pinks.

'Come in, Father.' She hurriedly closes out the world as she leads me into her sitting room. The room with the view of the street, a view I am sure she has watched evolve over the years. Her husband, bed ridden, upstairs took so much of her time that the seat by the window was a regular haunt for Agnes Thomson. The crucifix hanging on the wall spoke of religious observance and a devout adherence to a God who had left her in a hard life full of pain and duty.

'A terrible thing to happen.' I open with a starter to get her speaking. I know she needs to tell me something. If I make it easy for her she might just spill the lot quickly. At least she never felt the need for the mandatory tea offering. She shifted uneasily in her seat, looking once more at scene unfolding outside. The bin would be removed, body and all, with the extraction taking place in private at the morgue. It would eat up resources and tell us little more than I already knew.

'It is terrible.' She shook her head slowly from side to side, disbelief that this could be happening at her front door. 'I heard the bin lid banging down two nights ago. I had just given Bob a drink of water and was sitting here for a moment.' She looked over at me, deciding how much to reveal. I let her find my eyes and hold them, willing her to trust me with what she knew.

'He was a big man and he stomped down the street, a big dark coat pulled up with a hood. I couldn't see a face.' She looked away, screwing herself up a bit. 'I saw his hands dripping and I know now it was blood.' Her hand balling over her mouth as she realised what she had seen. 'I should have called the police then.' She seemed ashamed at her lack of action.

'We will find him. Thank you for telling me.' It hadn't been that much of a help but it did confirm the sequence of events. I patted her hand gently ' A police officer will get a proper statement soon.' She looked up at me, and pulled a deep shuddering breath inside to fuel her last snippet of information.

'When he got to the end of the street, I swear he

looked round and could see me watching. His eyes flared red in the dark. He was evil Father. And then he was gone.' She was terrified thinking he would return.

'He won't be back. Perhaps it was the light but I think you managed to see the evil that was in him.' I hold her hand, comforting her that she hadn't been seeing things. She was a devout soul and I was sure that faith would keep her warm at night. She had seen my demon but not the whole picture, luckily. The buzzer from upstairs told her that Bob needed her now.

Chapter 14

'It takes a great deal of strength to force a body in that space. I couldn't do it.' DI White was filling me in on the medical examiner's report. He had seen plenty in his time with the police but this was a first for him. I could feel the shock of it seeping from his pores. Sitting in his office, surrounded by folders full of paper on the cases on the whiteboards in the main room, I looked at him letting him continue. He knew we were chasing a demon but he still didn't really get it. His head was moving side to side in little micro movements as if his brain would not accept what he knew to be true.

'The Demon will be very strong and I doubt that it took much for it to snap her into that bin.' I had to remind him of what we faced. I suppose I could also have reminded him that there will be at least one more to be found and of course the final one on Sunday night. I decided that he didn't need that added on top of his shock. The medical examiner's report had included a line about the spinal injuries allowing compression into the space. That and the lack of internal organs. DI White nods; he's a little distracted.

The desk phone rings, pulling us back to the here and now and away from our own images playing in vivid colour in our heads. It might be easier if we could just project our thinking onto a wall or screen. I would bet on my show being the goriest. We look across the desk at each other, a moment where neither of us wants to pick up the phone, is this another scene discovered or someone upstairs demanding action. I raise my eyebrows, 'On you go' I might as well have said. A deep, sole of the boots, sigh escapes White as he lifts the handset.

'DI White.' A neutral, if a little tired, voice giving away nothing. His hands tightening on the handset the only clue of his feelings. The scrabbling hand finding a pen from the debris covering his desk and in a few seconds a terse 'go ahead' had him writing on a scrap of paper. The frown lines deepening as he made slashes with the pen. It was an address, apparently; I can read upside down. A skill that has surrendered many a secret to my eyes. I can do reflected, too, a man of many useful little skills. None of which are often that useful. I waited, the cool substance that covered the bottom of the Styrofoam cup was unappealing, until DI White caught my eye. He didn't really need to tell me that there was another body waiting for us.

'We have to go.' He managed to whisper. He was so close to defeat that he couldn't really summon a fight. I hoped he would recover from this. Cops see too many things that just hang around in their heads, waiting for a repeat like all the programmes on Dave. He looked up slowly finding my eyes, looking for a reassurance that I couldn't give him. This one might be as unforgettable as the one detailed on paper before us.

'We will get this bastard.' I tried to be confident but so far we were managing to lumber around in the Edinburgh traffic like a pair of drunk, blind men without a white stick between us. I don't think DI White was fooled. He stood up, pushing the chair back on its little castor wheels, it seemed that a huge bench press was needed to get upright. The weight of the world indeed.

White is getting the hang of this 'Flying Squad' thing; the blue lights and siren were deployed straight away. The interminable trips of stop-and-go were now replaced by a heavy right foot and the 'get-the-fuck-out-of-the-way' siren and lights combo. I didn't comment, I just held on to the handle for the afraid. The cars in the capitol seem to know how to make spaces that don't exist. Judicious use of the pavements to make a path between the tightest two lanes of traffic allows the emergency services to get through the old town in record time.

'Where are we going?' I ask, although I read the address, upside down, I had no actual idea where Perseus Crescent was. White needed to be distracted from his black fury that emanated from him, the crushing of the steering wheel looked almost painful.

'Leith.' He let it out and that was it. No other details. He seemed to be taking this personally, which might make him very volatile if we ever got our hands on the demon. It might make him dead. I couldn't have that; he was one of the good guys. I tried to remember the churches that were down Leith way but all that sprang to mind were the pubs and hookers that plied their trade there.

'St Thomas Aquinas.' I managed to pull one from my memory. It was a sturdy beast with a decent view over the sea. I couldn't recall who the Priest was; I could tell you who scored in the cup final of years gone by but the names of local priests was too difficult.

We were very nearly there and the abrupt halt and screaming of tyres caught me off guard, throwing me into the door as White had to swerve away from the arse end of a white transit van that didn't seem to hear or see our approach. DI White had obviously passed the advanced defensive driving course or had spent far too long racing karts at the indoor circuits. The collision that I thought was imminent was avoided with flicks of his wrists and fancy footwork.

'Get out of the way ya fucking arsehole!' He screamed at the top of his lungs as he swerved back in front of the startled van driver. I was holding on tight waiting for the crunch of metal but it never came. Our lights clearing the way as up ahead I could see the bell tower of St Thomas Aquinas. The grey skies beginning to offer the usual Lothian weather; a little moisture to help the grass and weeds grow.

The road ahead was full of police cars, an ambulance and a load of spectators trying to get a view over the yellow tape. We arrived just like the Sweeney, all screeching tyres and slamming doors. A

Uniformed constable raised the tape quickly to remove any delay. We were needed inside quickly. The clicking of cameras just one more noise in the cacophony. I was vaguely aware of a guy trying to ask DI White if this was the graveyard slasher.

Inside the church the milling about of white onesies meant that this was the crime scene. We moved like Moses, parting the red sea, and progressing into the vast church and taking in the High Altar and the stained glass that allowed multi-hued light to fill the space at any time of the day. I could smell the sweet, cloying smell of rotting flesh. It was nearby. The flash and clicking of a camera told me that a body was lying to the right but it was the body mounted on the cross that held my attention. It was like no one wanted to take him down. The gouges across his back a parody of the whip marks that adorned the back of Jesus as he bore his cross. The pile of rubble scattered all around witness to what had happened to the original cruciform of Christ. Hanging there now was a flesh and blood resident and from the shreds of clothing still clinging to him, it was the local priest. Father Francis, I recalled his name. I stepped up the central aisle, I think White was behind me but maybe he didn't want to approach the body hanging over the top of the cross. I couldn't really blame him.

I genuflect as I approached the rail and realised that it was probably not the right thing to do, after all the Crucifix had been defiled. The drips of blood that had made their way down the length of Father Francis back, thighs and shins were still intermittently adding to the pool below his blood covered feet. The splintered ruin of his shins showed that his killer had taken the time to torture him before he died. I moved around to see the front view and wished instantly that I hadn't.

Flapping from the ruin of his throat was his tongue. The black blood congealing and covering the purple shirt and white collar leaving a dark wet stain all over his chest. The mouth open in an eternal scream of pain and terror ringed in blood and home to a set of shattered teeth. Worst for me was the empty black and bloodied sockets where his kind eyes had once lived. I managed to avoid throwing up at the rivers of ichor and blood that had run from these sightless sockets. The destruction of Father Francis had been comprehensive and done as cruelly as possible, This was a killing for the pleasure of seeing another suffer.

A blurring of my sight as I stepped forward to touch his foot was due to the tears of genuine sadness for my brother in Christ. I let my finger tips touch his ankle, I am sure the onesie wearers were scandalised that I touched the body. I am ready for a hideous re-run of the last moments of Father Francis and the demonic fiend's orgiastic frenzy of cruelty. I let myself open to my gift. I feel the warmth travel up my arm as the waves of pain course through my body, echoes of the torment that Francis endured.

I often wish that I could fast forward past the pain, hurt and emotion like a DVD but I have to feel it all. The eyes, although removed are still allowing me to see and feel the wounds as they are inflicted. The end is pretty much as I expected and now I can see the scaled face of my enemy, his claws and his sharp incisor filled mouth. The cruelty in the eyes is like a blow with each glance. I watch as he entered this church, still wearing a human form. The body collapsing off in a heap as Father Francis stood screaming at the sight of the Demon emerging.

As it stalked slowly forward Francis had been unable to back away, frozen in place by the red eyed glare that held him. The disbelief of what was happening before him overwhelming his mind. Nothing really prepares you to see a demon peel its way out of a walking corpse. We have all seen the films but the actuality is much more shocking. I wondered what the medical staff would make of the remains, discarded in the pews.

DI White was moving towards me as I stepped away and let go. I must have looked awful, prompting him to ask if I was all right. I didn't want to explain that I had just felt a shadow of what Father Francis had, and to complain about it seemed disrespectful. I nodded but he guessed otherwise. He moved up towards the altar; he had to look. He was the commander on the scene now. I left him to it and sat on the front pew. How had the demon crossed the threshold and entered this house of God? It should have been enough to keep it out. Was it gaining in power with each death? Was the coming climax bringing it power? I had no idea.

I took out my phone fully intending to call the Bishop when he beat me to it. I almost dropped it as the vibrations pulsed in my hand. I quickly shut off the noise; I was sitting in a church after all.

'Steel.' Habits die hard, even though I knew it was

him and I needed his help. I still wouldn't give anything away.

'Andrew, are you at St Thomas Aquinas? The media are all over this.' His voice sounded hurried and a little frantic. I took a deep breath.

'Yes Bishop and it is carnage. Father Francis has been tortured and mounted on the cross by our demon. How it managed to walk in here I have no idea.' The peeling itself from the corpse could wait a few moments.

'There are television cameras on the way but there is a clip on the internet from a mobile phone.' That most certainly isn't my fault. I wondered what it had captured.

'What does it show? The demon left here in its own form I think.' Maybe Bishop Michael had watched it all.

'The video is a peek inside after the event and is moved on by a policeman. Still the fate of Father Francis is now circulating in lurid detail. The Home Secretary is most unhappy.' Bishop Michael passed on the dissatisfaction with aplomb. I think I am supposed to give a shit about the Home Secretary and his unhappiness, I don't.

'I have to go, DI White needs my help. I will call later.' I end the call before I get any more orders. I look up at White, he looks a little green about the gills. 'You all right?' I return the favour.

'We need to get Father Francis down from there and the remains bagged up.' I twitch my head over my shoulder. DI White signals a few of the onesies over and points at the body. They will have the logistical task of getting the body down. A blazing high power light has been set up outside, probably from the television crews, and it seems to flood the church with colours. The stained glass panels causing rainbows and patches of different coloured light to dance around us. I look sour but that isn't really a surprise as the Chief Superintendent stomps his way into the crime scene. The big outer door is slammed shut cutting off the hubbub from outside.

'DI White, update me on where we are.' Buttons tries not to bark but he manages not to stare at the body hanging over the cross. He fixes his gaze on White who starts to recount the very limited amount we know and makes it last longer than I could have done. Maybe White has a career in politics to look forward to.

'The press are out there like a pack of hyenas. I need more than that.' The Superintendent is as impressed with the long version as he would have been with my short 'Fuck knows' response. He has a funny puce colouring and I think he will look a bit flustered in front of the cameras.

'Right, we need to get the story straight. Is this the Graveyard slasher or is this a new psychopath?' He is barking now, and that never gets a great response. DI White looks to me to answer that one. Thanks mate, thanks a lot.

'It is the same person.' I manage to make it bland and give nothing away to the 'Brass' so that the more awkward questions are avoided. He hasn't been told the half of it and I doubt he could cope anyway. He's a square peg in square holes kind of guy.

'It seems that he's moved on from young women then. Are we sure?' We both nod, no point in pretending otherwise. 'White we will go out and give a holding statement. Father Steel you had better stay out of sight. We don't want to have you part of the circus. White, let's get this done. Formal briefing at Duke Street station in an hour or two.' Chief Superintendent Buttons knows how to cover ass and make the cameras focus on the right thing. He might as well have a 'nothing to see here sign made.' I doubt our brothers and sisters in the media will obey though.

Chapter 15

DC MacBride is left to provide any assistance I might need and to prevent my screwing things up. He is a decent, if somewhat spotty, cop and doesn't try to over reach. He takes a lot at face value from me and I expect that is more to do with the instructions from on high. He makes sure I am always within sight too, even when he is scribbling in his notebook. Perhaps he has been left to keep an eye on my unconventional activities and report back. Anyway as I walk around the church his eyes seem to be a constant companion.

The bodies have been bagged and taken to the morgue and will be examined tonight. I am still working to a Sunday night climax but my faith in Father Jeremy's predictions has taken a bit of a beating as the body count starts to rack up. So much for four or five. This demon has been a bit busier than that and we still have very little to go on. The patterns and randoms are inextricably tied up and we have no idea which is which. I wonder how the press briefing is going and how well DI White is managing to say we are devoid of clues,leads and the only thing we have a pile of is dead bodies.

'How did it manage to walk in here? It should never have managed to walk under the shadow of the Crucifix.' I realise I have spoken out loud. DC MacBride looks in my direction, as if wondering if it was aimed at him. I wave him back to his note taking as I walk around, letting the church speak to me. It isn't really saying much. I walk to the sanctuary lamp, its red glass diffusing the flame within, expecting something like inspiration to strike. It doesn't.

I sit on a smooth, varnished pew and let myself pray. Well, not exactly prayer, more a case of looks like prayer as I slip into a trance of sorts. I ease my will out into the church. It should feel sanctified and holy but this one feels null. Nothing. No spiritual energy; no holiness laid down over the years and years of delivering the sacrament to the Faithful. There is no feeling of faith suffusing the ground beneath our feet and no feeling of the enemy either. It is as if this church is not a Holy place at all.

'Jeremy. It's Andrew. I am in St Thomas Aquinas in Leith. It doesn't feel right. Can you look into the history of the place.' I speak quickly knowing that he will have a long set of questions to illicit my 'For Fucks Sake' response. I am hoping for a quick dismount and escape.

'Yes it is the place you are seeing on the news. Our friend walked in here and killed the priest. Bold as brass. I have to go. Let me know.' I click end call. I am getting too like Bishop Michael. Aye right.

It is like an itch on the inside of my brain. The need to know and I has left me in serious trouble at times. I walk to the entrance vestibule and start my walk from there. The oak doors, so solid and studded with iron, at my back keeping the night out as I step forward on the smooth grey flagstones. They are well worn and old, not some modern addition or laminate flooring that seems to find its way into modern churches. The font ahead of me, beautifully sculpted, with a decent level of water in the bowl. I place my hand on the stone, letting my mind open to the holiness that should emanate from it. It doesn't give anything. No power of the Lord in this font. It might as well be a thirty quid sink from Homebase.

I know I am looking grumpier by the minute. I start to recite the Lord's Prayer, bringing something holy into this empty place. I speak softly so that my words fall in a shroud around me, no one else needs to hear me. The words tumbling in a stream from my lips fly straight to God's ear; or at least that is what we tell people. The rites, repeated every weekday and twice on Sunday have been washed away. The footsteps of this demon have cast years of devotion aside. How it has managed this I have no idea but I am afraid. The Priest who stood before the demon was afraid and it seemed to embolden the beast. Memories of his screams of torment rattle about inside my head as I walk the stations of the cross.

    This isn't a case of satanic squatters and a front of a church; this is a case of the church being totally wiped of any sanctity. I continue on, praying and blessing at each cardinal point; praying at the little side shrines, Hail Mary-ing and Our Fathering repeatedly as my fingers run over the beads of the rosary. There is no resistance to my words or deeds and that is heartening. Standing at the altar, I open my spirit and 'feel' my way over it. The blood splatters have not been cleaned yet and, while it looks a bit gory, it is just a block of stone. The whole church will need re-sanctified and reconsecrated, the Bishop will need to arrange that once the furore and circus moves on.

'I have to head back to base Father. Do you want a lift?' DC MacBride calls to me from about as far away as he can be. He is uncomfortable being in here and not because of the bodies that have been removed. He's seen too many exorcist movies I'd bet and knows what happens to the sidekicks and help.

'I will be fine here. I have some thinking to do and I will see DI White in the morning at the task force room.' I don't look over my shoulder. The crazy priest is staying and he is glad to be going. To be honest I am glad he is going too, his watching me like an informant was becoming a little tedious. I notice the television camera's are still here but they aren't lighting the church up any more, just a hubbub and smaller individual spotlights for the 'live from the scene' pieces. They will be running this all night and tomorrow I expect.

A thought, you know the creepy undermining kind of 'what if' thoughts, struck me. What if it didn't leave? What if it was still here somewhere? I wonder what the first on scene officers did by way of a check? Shit. It wasn't in here but I couldn't tell if it was still hiding on the grounds or in the bell tower. This place is such a null, I can't feel very much at all. I need to find out. The oak and iron studded door is shut and I know there is a uniformed policeman outside but I really don't want to be caught on camera opening the door and calling him in. Discrete the Bishop had said; this might not be discrete at all if it is still here.

I pull the door open about three inches and peek around the edge like Harold Lloyd, ridiculous and silly but I spy the uniform and psst him over. He takes a moment before he gets that I want him to come inside. Maybe I needed to wave at him or something, so far so good no action from the camera crews. I slip the door closed, quietly.

'Officer was a full search of the building done on arrival?' The puzzled and not very helpful look tells me that maybe full and search didn't take place. I try again. 'Can you radio in and find out?' I don't want to scream but he really isn't keeping up. My terseness can get out of hand if things don't go my way, escalating into a full strop and toys out the pram behaviour. I wait as he radios through my question. We stand together waiting on the reply. A noise from far inside reaches our ears. I don't need to wait for the answer, I know.

'Get DI White and back up, now.' I shove him towards the door as I head past the font of totally normal water and into the tennis court sized playing field that the Demon has already played on. My footsteps ringing out as I stomp across the stone floor, I am coming and it knows it. A fury building in my chest as I recall the cruelty visited on Father Francis a reason for my headlong pursuit of a demon that might just rip my head off and spit in the hole.

'Flee as you will, the vengeance of the Lord follows you.' My voice like a sergeant major's as he roars commands to recruits on his parade ground. The sounds of flight fill the church ahead of me, the scrape of talons on the stone steps of the bell tower, telling me that my enemy has no where to run. My crucifix presented boldly before me as proof of which side I am on and the only weapon I have with me. That and Faith, obviously.

'Run ya bastard, I am coming.' Not very ritualistic but I want to get my hands on this one. The brutal murders of Brenda, Caroline and the rest making the red mist descend, and caution well and truly a long forgotten thing. I start to mount the bell tower steps, my knees pumping as the first few corners pass in a blur but the tightness in my chest starts to slow me up as oxygen isn't being sucked deep into my lungs. At this rate I couldn't catch the thirty nine bus let alone a demon fleeing the wrath of God.

The last few turns are abject agony as my knees scream at their treatment and my lungs burn from the abuse I put them through. There ahead of me is an abomination that should never have been in our world; a scaled red and black skinned murdering bastard. The sharp rows of teeth that have been buried in human flesh so vicious looking, a warning not to get too close. The snarl on lizard like lips and the hiss of warning as I step on to the bell platform, it is wary. It would be better if it was afraid, then I might have an advantage.

'I abjure you, in the name of Our Lord Jesus Christ.' I step forward, my arm steady and the silvered-iron crucifix boldly presented. The flinch away from my words and symbol fill me with a hope that warms me to my core. The demon moves in a blur of movement swinging the bell hard on the rocker. In a second I am bowled across the small space into the stone wall, crucifix falling from my fingers as the numbness travels down my arm and causes my fingers to spasm in pain. I stare up at the demon, relieved to see the back not the descending teeth that might have ended my life in a bloody fountain as it ripped my throat from the front of my neck. The shattering of the louvre slats under a heavy fist making a portal through which it was about to depart. The wings unfurling as it flew into the darkness of the night.

'Aye run ya bastard.' I manage to mutter before the coughing and wincing commences. What on earth was I thinking? Rambo I am most certainly not.

Chapter 16

I know that I should have waited for back up. Really though, how would have back up been any use in the bell tower? If White had been with me he might have been the victim of a slash of wicked talons leaving him bleeding to death as his arteries pumped his life's blood all over the walls of the bell tower. The pain in my shoulder is a small, but worthwhile, price to pay to get close to the enemy. I can identify it now to Father Jeremy, whom I expect to have a rogues gallery to interrogate and thereafter a solution as to how to defeat it. After all, he is meant to be the fount of all knowledge.

'Father Steel.' An unknown voice is yelling up the stairwell. I presume it is the uniformed cop from the front door. He sounds a bit panicked. Maybe they were told to protect me.

'I am up here.' I manage to shout back and start the process of getting up from my supine position lying where the bell left me. I doubt anything is broken but that doesn't mean the groaning and wincing is any less. I hear him climbing the stairs and he doesn't sound like breathing is a problem, even with the kevlar vest and the tool belt bigger than batman.

His head appears round the corner and he scans the platform, seeing nothing but a smashed out louvre and the priest trying to rise from the floor. He moved up into the small space, his night stick a pointless implement in his hand, what he thought he would do with it is beyond me. He helps me to my feet, muttering concerned sounds and not commenting on the, rather impressive, coating of dust that has transformed my black uniform.

'Let's go.' I don't try to explain what has happened. One less person to swear to secrecy and one less for the Bishop to berate me about. The lack of comprehension covering his face is comical and if each step down the stairwell hadn't been a juddering pain I might have found it humorous. As it was, I was in a great deal of discomfort by the time I had parked my sweaty ass on the front pew. I sent him back to his post outside and I waited for DI White to appear to be told how much of a fuck up, we had contributed to.

I sent a text to Jeremy while I sat there, recovering. I could almost see him ecstatic at the news I could identify the 'other-worlder' and had a decent description. Almost like donkey in the kids cartoon Shrek, jumping up and down almost wetting himself.

The beep was a little too quick, Jeremy had replied. A few flurries of thumbs and we had arranged to meet at the seminary tonight. The joy of joys that was my evening to come. I would need to imbibe if I was to avoid committing a crime with a lengthy prison term.

I was on my second glass of Château something-or-other and reclining on my bed, letting the ache in my shoulder ease away on a raft of alcoholic anaesthetic when Jezza opened my door. He managed to look excited and bookish at the same time, an arm full of folders was trying to escape as he tried to shut the door. Almost with a final bid for freedom the four shiny black plastic folders slipped from his grasp and fell on to the foot of the bed. A look of relief on his face that they hadn't cascaded to the floor spilling their contents as the ring bindings popped open.

'Father Andrew, how are you this evening?' He was trying to catch his breath after his exertions with the folders. I poured him a glass of wine and let him get settled.

'These folders contain pictures of Demons through the ages and are compiled from many different sources. I thought that you might be able to pick out the one most like the adversary you fought tonight. It might give us some clues on how to combat it.' He swigged his wine a little quickly for my thinking; maybe he was fortifying himself.

I opened the first cover and looked at the depiction; a five year old with a crayon could have produced better. It was going to be a long night if the artwork was going to be like this all the way through. Jeremy said nothing helpful as I tried, and succeeded, in not snorting derisively. The pictures carried on in a similar vein for a while, all being extracted from very old looks by the look of them. Soon though they started to improve a little and I am sure I passed one that looked remarkably like Milton's paradise lost. The first folder was finished and I didn't think there was much to say about the contents that wouldn't sound like a churlish teenager so I started the second after refilling our glasses. I would need to open another bottle on the next round.

The second must have been more recent, if the nineteenth century is more recent, and the lithographs were much better. More detail and much more realistic. Gone were the childlike representations and instead the images were obviously authentic. Little details and feelings that left me in no doubt that those making these images had seen them not just imagined and fantasised about them. Some of the artists had caught the malice in the looks too, which made them seem to leap of the page and would have been frightening to those of their time.

I look up at Jezza, a bit grudgingly perhaps but I meant it 'These are good, much better than I expected after the early ones.' He smiled and nodded, his wine coming dangerously near to spilling for my liking.

'Thanks, it has taken a while to compile. I have kept all the really speculative rubbish out and focussed on the ones that are authenticated or match other texts. I have an identikit pack that we can use if the gallery doesn't work.' Jeremy was prepared for the eventuality that I couldn't pick out a likeness. Bless him.

The pages turn more slowly now as I start to pick

out features and likenesses that bear some resemblance to what I faced tonight but nothing is quite right or even that close. I wondered if the search would be like trying to identify one sheep in a flock of thousands; I know they say shepherds can tell each one apart but I doubt that is really that true. I lift my glass absently to my lips and a disappointed sigh escapes as I realise it is empty. I put it down again and am pleasantly surprised to see Jezza fish a bottle from his man bag. It looks expensive and not a cheap one from Tesco either.

'I brought a little refreshment. Looking through these folders is thirsty work.' He smiles and deftly opens the bottle, handling the corkscrew like an old hand. As he pours he tells me that there is a great little vintner (off licence to you and me) just around the corner from his lodgings and some real bargains can be had if you know what to look for. Who knew he was a connoisseur of the fermented grape? I taste the luxurious red liquid and decide that his shop needs a visit.

An hour passes until my close encounter fills a page before me. The picture is black and white but there is no doubt that this is my guy or at least one of is relatives. I look up at Jeremy.

'This is it. The one I chased was red and black but this is our guy.' I pass the folder to Jeremy letting him peer down through his reading glasses to get a good look. It also freed up my hands to refill from the very tasty red wine that had my name on it. I sat back, pleased that the whole exercise hadn't been a total bust and that Jeremy had been decent company too. He was reading the three pages of notes behind the depiction and muttering to himself as he absorbed the bio of the enemy. I was a little too fuzzy to do that so I waited to be told the highlights.

'This bad boy has been around.' Jeremy swigged his glass obviously enjoying the taste before carrying on. At least he didn't swirl, gargle and spit it out. 'He has been recorded a number of times in the last two centuries but the image comes from a body of work by a parapsychologist in Paris, Pierre Tourand. He has had regression therapy patients produce images very like this on a number of occasions. They have been remarkably consistent to be honest.' He pauses for effect and carries on with the background. 'It is unusual for multiple patients to describe the same thing in isolation, lending authenticity to their stories.

They are each independent of each other and have no contact.'

'That is all very well and good Jeremy, but I need to know what to expect when I meet it again and, more importantly, how to banish it from here.' I try to keep him on track with his musings. I know that it is real and not an imaginary demon encounter having been close to it now on two separate counts.

'We think it is summoned for a short spell to complete a specific task lasting a whole lunar month. The notes suggest that it makes recreation of its time in our world delaying completion of the task until the last possible moment.' He looks over his glasses at me, all serious and scholarly. 'That might explain the extra kills and seeming randomness. It also means we have some surety that this spree will end on Sunday night at the latest.'

'Does it have a name?' I ask, not really sure why it matters but it might. Jeremy seems surprised that I asked.

'There are a few names listed but none are authenticated. The most occurring is for Basomel.'

Chapter 17

Ideas that strike at three in the morning are generally not the greatest and should, in the cold light of day, be discarded. This one was probably no exception. I had been thinking about how to find the demon's lair, or rather Basomel's lair, and had struck on the idea of the tourist bus that flits around the old town of Edinburgh. The bus is a hop on, hop off arrangement but I planned just to sit on the open top deck and feel if there were any traces or spots that needed more attention. I would sort of zone out and see what turned up. I did, however, need company and Father Jeremy had agreed to meet me and be my chaperone. I think he just wanted to be involved in the hunt for the Demon.

Starting at the world famous Scott Monument we climbed aboard and paid the twenty quid for the experience. Unlimited travel for the day on the route which seemed bloody steep to me and would probably be mostly unused. If we didn't find it today then we were screwed for tomorrow night the mission, whatever it was, would be completed and Basomel would be on his way back to the pit that spawned him. We were on the clock, as it were.

Father Jeremy had brought a Thermos and some sandwiches to 'keep us going' but I doubted the contents of the flask would be any more drinkable than Murdoch's coffee. I had pre-stocked myself with two Danish pastries before meeting Jeremy. The paper cup of rapidly cooling Costa latte was keeping my fingers warm and making me regret the lack of my gloves. We sat at the front of the double decker bus, enjoying the shield of the windscreen but still outside in the fresh air. I wasn't cold yet, but I was sure I would be before too long. The incipient hangover was threatening to return as my early morning paracetamol was wearing off.

We were off, and the smooth ride advertised was relative to being in the back of an army truck. The juddering stop start of the capitol traffic was down to the tram building project and not the driver's fault, or at least so he said. I put it down to his lack of clutch control and a past it, old bus. However, the slow weaving through the Old Town was what we wanted and soon I had slipped into my waking zombie routine.

The coffee, long since finished, left me holding a soggy paper cup that needed to be disposed of.

I waited, open and receptive to any trace of our quarry but nothing much was forthcoming. Maybe being on the bus was too far from being able to feel him. Usually I would be able to pick it out of the tapestry of the city. After all I had danced with him twice now and relived his finest handiwork repeatedly; there should be a stronger link.

Crossing over the North Bridge on our way to the Royal mile and the Palace of Holyrood, I felt a vague unease but that could have been anything and I made a mental note to probe more on the next pass over the bridges. The Train Station sits below with the mass of people and buildings nestled under the main arches. I like the cobbled Royal Mile as it passes all the twee Jockanese shops selling tartan everything and tat imported from China and they sit cheek by jowl with traditional pubs and kilt makers. It is a real hotch-potch of shops and experiences. The street performers earning their meagre crusts attract tourists in crowds and the locals even stop to watch, occasionally. It is all part of what makes Edinburgh so much more appealing than Glasgow. Cultural festivals are embedded now and it has begun to pull in visitors from all over the globe. Although if we don't catch this demon then perhaps the tourists won't return.

In what seemed like a blink of an eye we were down to the Palace and the new, over budget, parliament building that had just needed even more work done on its security. After all the main chamber was right over the entrance and a car bomb would have been particularly effective. Of course, when the design was approved we didn't need to worry about that sort of thing. It is an interesting building when viewed from the air, or Arthur's Seat but from the street it was totally underwhelming. Four hundred and fifty million quid not so well spent I think most people felt. Anyway I felt nothing down here and we had a ten minute halt.

'What's on the sandwiches?' I spoke without preamble and scared Jeremy out of his skin. He would be a great help if we got into a scrape. He smiled nervously and handed me a cheese, tin foil wrapped, sandwich.

After an hour and a half we were going round again, sandwiches consumed and the beginning of a need for a comfort break was becoming more insistent. Then it happened. I was trying to pay attention as we crossed the North Bridge and I felt a pull that could only mean below us. I got up and dragged a startled Jeremy from the bus at the next available stop; the junction of the Royal Mile and the Bridges. We had a lead. It seemed my crazy tourist idea had turned out to be not so daft after all. Well hopefully I could pinpoint the location of Basomel and we, Father Jeremy and I, could deal with it.

In my pockets I had three vials of Holy water, my crucifix and some dead sea salt; Jeremy was similarly tooled up. We would be well equipped to meet Basomel; especially in the daylight. We walked down the knee killer Fleshmarket close and its stone steps worn down by years of revellers. The Halfway House pub would need to be missed this time, although I had been in there on more than one drunken occasion.

With a little regret at missing out on a pint and a growing feeling of going in the right direction my aching knees carried me down through the dim alley to the main road below. I am just pleased to be going down the steps and not up. Although I have gone the other way more than once and needed oxygen by the time I reached the middle let alone the top.

Market street and the back of the train station lay before me the chill wind and noisy traffic made me pull my coat tighter; I was cold and I hoped it was just the weather. Jeremy was buttoning his coat too, at least his looked substantial, mine was a bit thin. Out of season and pretty much useless for the frigid air of autumn Edinburgh. I felt the pull to my left The high North Bridge above us to the right, all sooty and showing signs of the years of train emissions.

'Let's go.' I muttered to my companion as I stepped smartly across the road between little gaps in the slow moving traffic. I hoped Jeremy knew how to cross the road and not get run over; if he wasn't a city boy he might struggle.. He followed me closely and that might be a good thing at some point. Moving on past a few galleries and boutiques I saw where I was being led.

'You've got to be kidding me.' I stopped abruptly causing a neat body swerve from Jeremy. He was looking round a little confused. 'Look.' I know I sounded sour but I couldn't really help it. Ahead of us on a black sign the words in dripping blood red 'The Edinburgh Dungeon' was our destination.

A theme park of the macabre history of Edinburgh

with full sounds, sights and smells to make the visit authentic feeling. Well, if my senses were right, it would be a very authentic experience. I doubt that it was hiding in here all the time but it might explain why no one reported seeing something on the streets.

Jeremy laughed, a little too shrill in my ears, before he asked 'What do we do now?' I am pleased he thought I should know and a bit irritated that I had no clear idea on what to do. My bladder was sending me a warning that the cold and coffee had contributed to its need to be relieved. Being cold isn't my favourite thing and needing a pee isn't high on the list either, I shrugged answering my bladder and Jeremy.

'Lets get a coffee and think about this. If it is in there, we can't have it being publicly exposed and causing pandemonium. The Bishop would have an aneurysm.' I start moving back to the train station making sure that Jeremy is right beside me. If I get too close it may know I am coming. It might feel our approach and bolt. We wouldn't want that now would we.

Chapter 18

Stirring my latte and enjoying the post bladder relief sensations had given me time to think. Jeremy was on the phone to the Bishop and I think he was finding out that his news was not well received. Bishop Michael did not need, nor did he really want the details. He wanted us to solve the problem and do it discretely. It was the discretely bit that I usually failed on. I could hear the 'yes Bishop, No Bishop, three bags full Bishop from over here.' We weren't in uniform but I doubt anyone was fooled by Jezza's disguise of being a normal.

I have been in the dungeon, years ago, and it wasn't a great idea. The effigies of the macabre gain their own power as more and more people look at them and feel fear. Burke and Hare were fine but some of the other attractions were beginning to absorb and would need some attention in the future.

The torturer and his set are particularly authentic and I could hear screams and echoes of a past that hadn't really happened just been acted out time and time again. I wasn't looking forward to going inside. The tours have a guide and take you through the various attractions as a group which might make dealing with Basomel a bit tricky.

Of Course, I am assuming he is hiding in plain sight, like an exhibit he could be hiding in the back or in their storage areas.

'Bishop Michael has left it to us to deal with. Discretely.' Jeremy is a bit breathless as he sits down. I'd bet his Americano with hot, skimmed, milk is cold and undrinkable but that's his own problem. I'd have had my coffee first, before beginning to check in with his Eminence.

'Of course he does.' Sarcasm is seeping out again. Jeremy swigs the cold sludgy coffee and his face cheers me right up again. He is deciding if spitting it out is better than swallowing it. He has such good manners he swallows it, keeping his complaint internalised.

'Here's my plan. We buy two tickets and join the tour. When we find him we hang back and, in the gap between the tours, we drive him off. Simples' I pretend I am the meerkat from the insurance advert. Great plan I think.

'What if he..' My hand silences him and again when he tries to restart with another question. 'But..' He isn't buying into the plan.

'Jeremy, we can't plan much more than that as we have no idea what we will find in there. If the tour doesn't reveal him then we need to see what our options are.' I am condescending, talking to a child who understands nothing and worries too much.

'What do you have with you? I have Holy water, dead sea salt and my crucifix. You?' I speak quietly, not wanting to draw any more attention than Jeremy's call to the Bishop did a few moments before.

'Holy water, the Host, a jar of Unction and my Crucifix.' Jeremy is seems is packing heat or hunting demon bear. I wonder if I am a little underprepared or lacking in weaponry. Too late now. We will just have to manage; two holy gunslingers heading to the saloon.

It takes less than five minutes to be standing in a queue of tourists waiting for the next group tour. It seems to be very busy and the queue moves so slowly. Groups of twelve are being led away at ten minute intervals and we will be in the next one with eight far eastern visitors and two Americans who seem rather taken with my surly Scots accent and Jeremy's plummy one. They have lots of cameras slung around their necks let alone the number of smartphones, if things get a bit hairy keeping things under wraps might be a bit difficult. Oh the Bishop will be pleased.

'Next group, move forward please.' A polite costumed tour guide, who must be an acting student, theatrically waves us forward. Jeremy and I gravitate towards the back behind Sam the American and his wife Tanya, they are nice people to be fair but I want them to give us a bit of room. We are moving towards the famous pair of grave robbers Burke and Hare, hearing of their heinous crimes in lurid and gasp-inducing details.

I can feel 'our friend' has been in here, more than many places but I have no real idea if he is here now. It isn't an exact science and sometimes I just feel something that is from the past more than I expect. We are heading into another exhibit about cannibals in caves I think, I wasn't really listening but the cave constructions are very realistic and perhaps I need to wander round the corner away from the area subtly lit by floor and ceiling coloured faders. I pull Jeremy back with me as we let the others move on a bit. His eyes are looking a bit wide and wired, no more coffee for him, as I pull him into the shadow of the glass fibre cave stone. A finger to my lips in the universal shut the fuck up' and I lead us into the shadows.

In a few steps the darkness is nearly complete as the mock cave turns a corner, taking us away from the main path through the planned historical attractions. I let my eyes get used to the near darkness, if it is here we might be in trouble if we can't see. I have my little mag-lite torch in my pocket and as I can still see absolutely nothing I decide to get it out. The cone of bright white light shows an empty corridor leading to a fire exit. I click it off and we turn to catch up with the group.

Our guide has come looking for us and is none too happy at our dalliance with the way out and not having been rapt in his delivery about the sinister side of Edinburgh history. He urges us to keep up as we make a move for the next bit. I wonder what he thought we were doing. I wonder if he thinks we are a couple? You know, like the Birdcage or something like that. He manages to stay in character, spinning out the fake 'auld scots' that nobody has uttered seriously for decades; I wonder if I suffer from the Scottish cringe. I don't think so; I just have no tolerance to shite and am a grumpy old man in training. Anyway we mince back to the rest of the group and their disapproval for holding up the fright-fest.

The interminable nonsense continues as we parade through an eighteenth century operating theatre, a court that ordered some woman to be hanged and apparently they heard her banging on the coffin after the event and decided the sentence had been carried out and she was allowed to go. 'Huaf hingit Mary' or as the guide explained it was 'Half Hanged Mary' and the understanding dawned on our tourist friends from the land of the rising sun. Personally I thought it just showed that the council was piss poor in those days too.

We were past the worst, or was it the best bits, when I could feel him. He was close by; I doubted that he was in another body it felt so raw. I knelt down to tie my lace, letting Jeremy move a step past me while I let my mind wander around us. I slipped my hand into my pocket and slowly removed a vial of Holy water. 'He is very close' I whispered letting Jeremy know that the action was about to kick off. I stood up and turned round looking behind us. I could feel him, watching, waiting and hoping we would walk on by.

I waved my hand in an arc splashing a little sizzling rain of Holy water across the space I thought was where he was hidden. His scream, like a rasping howl across a violin, filled the tight space we filled. He had managed to mask his visible presence but not the essence of his being. The Holy water had dispelled everything racking his body with searing pain. The light in this transition corridor was low and the red and black skin, fangs and red eyes were less distinct, fortunately. I criss crossed another two slashes from my vial causing agonised screams to fill the air as he turned and fled.

Jeremy and I were in hot pursuit as we tried to corner the beast although it moved faster than an Olympic sprinter. I heard the push bar fire exit clatter open as we turned the corner. The screams filling the corridors behind us would need to be sorted out later. We emerged from the caves into a storage space and cafeteria which had a trail of scattered chairs and tables telling us which way it had fled. It was outside and getting away. There are many shady alleys and passages in the Old town area of Edinburgh and if we didn't catch up soon it would disappear right in front of us.

'Jeremy call White, we need him down here as soon as he can.' I shout directions over my shoulder as I burst out into the street. Chaos has descended on the street. A taxi is at ninety degrees across the road and the traffic is a total shambles. There are screamers and a few stunned looking pensioners as well as a few kids with their phones taking it all in.

I shout 'Which way?' my crucifix is in my hand as I try to sprint. The alley is dim at best and dark in many places but I doubt it has stopped. It is fleeing the scene and no doubt has a few places to hide around here.

A scream from the end of the alleyway tells me that I am behind but the daylight is slowing it, or at least I hope it is. My arms are pumping like a madman and I don't think I can keep running at this pace for much longer. I am a middle aged man not made for running and my shoes aren't exactly helping.

I charge out of the alleyway and see the stunned surprised faces looking to my right so I head right. After all a large, cloaked red and black skinned beast has just run up the street and into another alley (they are called closes here) and I am trying to find breath to tell people to get the fuck out of my way. It comes out a little like 'Excuse me', it is that good mannered Britishness that infests me at times. The close is downhill a little making it easier than an uphill one, but there is no sign of the bastard, I am way behind and I am soaked with sweat. There seemed to be little real surprise or panic among those who were witnesses to the demon; perhaps they thought it part of the Fringe or something. Certainly no screaming and panic. What is wrong with these people?

Chapter 19

Red faced, breathless and bent double trying not to throw up is how DI White found me at the end of the close. I had the presence of mind to put the crucifix away so that the nice people of Edinburgh and their tourist friends were not alarmed by a man charging about brandishing a cross I front of him. My breathing was slowly beginning to work and the pain in my knees was almost unbearable.

'You okay?' I recognised his voice or I might have just waved him off. I looked up through my sweaty fringe and nodded, wasn't it obvious that I was just peachy? I nodded again and pushed up from my knees and leaned back against the wall. 'What happened?' He asked, I just wondered what Jeremy's message had been. A garbled mess most likely.

'It was hiding in the Dungeon.' As if that should be explanation enough. Or perhaps that was all the breath I had to use. DI White needed more than that though, after all the chaos caused by the initial part of the chase took a little cleaning up. The police switchboard had gotten a little busy about a large cloaked figure being chased by a middle aged man.

'Father Jeremy and I found it and caused it to flee. I chased it but it can run faster than I can. Fucker got away. It could have gone to ground around here or kept going.'

'We need to search the area. It could still be here. The place is mobbed and it could be carnage.' He is taking it seriously, which is good, discrete it will not be. What is he going to say? We are looking for a large bulky demon in a black cloak with jagged teeth and red and black skin?

'We need to be discrete. These things are best done quietly.' I try to stand straight but it is a challenge. 'It would be better to call it a stunt by students or something. It isn't beyond the realms of possibility'

He doesn't seem at all convinced but we will keep the search to a couple of uniforms and White and myself. Oh yes and Father Jeremy.

'Andrew, I have just seen video of you running up the royal mile with your crucifix waving about. What on earth is going on? The Home Office are having a fit.' Bishop Michael is on the phone and unusually his manners have slipped. He seems a little put out. I can't imagine why.

'I was chasing the Demon up the street.' I am being childish and I am sure he knew that. I wait for the outburst before I continue, an outburst that doesn't come. I can almost see his pursed lips and frown deepening as he sits behind his desk.

'What about being discrete? I expected better from you.' His disappointment attack would work on most people but not on me. I don't really worry about being a disappointment; I am immune these days having disappointed so many on so many occasions. My mother probably over used the approach when I was a child building up my resistance to it.

'It was hiding out in the Edinburgh Dungeon when we discovered it. I splashed him with Holy water and it fled the scene.' Oh dear I have been hanging around the police too long; next it will be proceeding along the road. 'It was better to chase it than to let it run I thought.'

'In the Dungeon? Really? That is remarkable. Well, yes you probably did the right thing driving it out of there but waving your crucifix in the air and shouting and swearing at people to move? That was not acceptable Andrew.' A demon is running loose killing priests and young women and my swearing is unacceptable? I count to ten because I can feel a 'Fuck off' rolling on my tongue and it had better not get out. I take the necessary deep breath and let it out before the safer response of 'Yes Bishop' escapes my lips.

'We could always say it was a tester for a film? Most people seemed to think it wasn't real anyway. They stood and gawped rather than flee screaming.' Limiting the exposure on this was going to be vital and I thought this was better than the student stunt but it isn't really my area.

'I think I could get that to work Andrew, that's a good cover. Is Father Jeremy still with you? Tell him well done on identifying the Other-worlder. Keep me posted.' And just like that I was dismissed.

We were still wandering around the upper section of the Royal mile when DI White handed me my third paper cup of coffee; it must have been my round but I missed it. We were cold and footsore and it was dark. The lights made up for a great deal, being so pretty and everything however our overwhelming failure to find hide nor hair of the enemy was frustrating. The area around us was filled with marks of its passing and there were many of them. This must have been the centre of its activity, if the frequency was anything to go by.

I swigged and scalded my tongue and managed not to swear but I saw DI White smirk at my misfortune. I rubbed at my tongue and I suppose that made me look even sillier but it seemed to work. DI White did an update on his radio and received two negative responses from our uniformed helpers.

'If I wanted a showy finale to my mission where around here would I do it?' I mused aloud. Sometimes I ask decent questions when I talk to myself. Jeremy turned to look at me as if I had sprouted a pair of horns, an odd look on his face. Well, an odder look than usual.

'Basomel is a show off so that is a good question. Tomorrow night he will complete his mission at midnight. He will need holy ground and this area is right in the eye of his storm.' Jeremy was getting scholarly and all excited, bless him.

'I think you are right but where would he chose?' I wanted an answer not a lecture. I was still trying to get my scalded tongue to calm down so I could have more coffee.

'Behind you.' DI White spoke quietly between non scalding sips. We both looked round at him like he was speaking gibberish. He flicked his head to the building right behind us. St Giles Cathedral standing proudly ignored behind us. It was resplendent in the lights of the Royal Mile. After years of grime and traffic soot build up, it had been shot blasted clean and looked relatively new.

'Would it try there Jeremy? What about the Tron just down there or that one up the road?' It was Edinburgh and I could see churches round almost every corner but St Giles is the Cathedral, so maybe.

'The Cathedral would be the ultimate desecration and two fingers.' Jeremy nodded and DI White seemed to be willing to take him seriously. It was thin and based on a random question that I asked myself, very thin.

'Wouldn't hurt to take a look. I can arrange it for tomorrow.' DI White was right, it wouldn't hurt but I thought it might be a total waste of time that we couldn't afford. Would he strike again tonight, it being his last hurrah before the climax? I doubted that he would after all the criss cross of Holy water would have seared to his very soul.

'Lets do that. We need to make sure that we have enough eyes out and about tonight though.' I was unsure that having more uniforms patrolling would make any difference but at least it would keep the Chief Superintendent happy. Something must be done and all that.

'It must be my round. Pint lads?' I make the universal pint swigging gesture and I get two takers for my offer. This being Edinburgh, the one thing we have an abundance of is pubs and luckily they are always close to the churches. Is there a causal link there? I believe that there might be. I always need a pint after church and it seems that the men and women of Edinburgh feel the same.

Chapter 20

Waking up in a strange bed and not being too sure about how I got there is not a usual thing for me. I know I was with DI White so I doubt I got into too much trouble. Father Jeremy left early in the evening citing a need to do some research but I think he was struggling to keep up. We were talking shop for most of the evening when PC Jill and MacBride turned up and kept us company. I look over and a half dressed DI White is lying on the other side of the double bed, I can smell bacon cooking and when I move my head I am a little fuzzy but not totally defeated by a hangover, so rough just about sums it up. Not the rough as guts, just rough.

I pull myself to my feet finding my socks still on and my trousers over the chair. I am a middle aged man and the morning after sight is not a great one. I pull my trousers on and stagger to the bathroom. I look in the mirror, a little bleary, not too bloodshot and after the mandatory cold water facelift I feel much more human. I rub some toothpaste in my mouth and swirl with the tap water, thank goodness the foul taste has gone.

'Morning.' I shuffle along the corridor to the living room and find Jill has slept on the couch, giving up her bed for the two old boys. She pops her head out of the kitchen and smiles.

'Morning Father, Would you like tea or coffee? The bacon wont be long.' She is such a bright morning person she is making my head hurt. I am grateful though.

'Coffee would be great. Paracetamol would be good too, if you have some.' The need to clear my head is taking precedent over any other function. Caffeine and painkillers are always a good start. DI white shambles in to the room, much more worse for wear than I am. He looks terrible, serves him right for getting us both pissed. I am ensconced on the couch sitting on the quilt that had been used last night by the very generous PC Jill. She had let the pair of drunk old blokes pass out in her bed and made the use of the couch, which felt very comfortable.

DI White is a groaner. Every movement is accompanied by a little noise and a subsequent holding of his head. He is a bit of a scratcher too, although his hand doesn't stray to his bollocks. A fact for which I am eternally grateful. He shuffles on to the couch and catching my eye, gives a chuckle of embarrassed camaraderie. Now that we have gotten pissed together there is a bond that can't be broken; or at least that is the drunken theory.

Jill hands out coffee and didn't even bat an eye at the state of semi dress that is her senior officer. The pain killers are consumed and plates of bacon rolls appear; either she is truly a generous hostess or she wants us to get lost. I don't get any feeling that we are being booted out. I wonder what her boyfriend would think of two colleagues crashing at her place after an extended impromptu session.

'Is Sandy coming over Jill?' DI White asks her round the side of his buttery bacon roll. He obviously knows more about Jill than I do, I never thought to ask last night or if I did I promptly forgot.

'About ten, we have church this morning. There's plenty of time though so don't panic.' She sipped her mug of tea. She started to tidy up around us as we started to return to the land of the living emerging from the Sunday morning clan of post-binge zombies.

'I need to go home and call in. The Bishop will

want to know what we will be doing to resolve the problem. Tonight will be busy. Can you get the men to stake out the targets?' I slurp my coffee like a truck-stop cafe customer; following it with a chunk of bacon roll.

DI White is nodding in agreement, so all will be well then. I leave the details to him to sort out with the Chief Superintendent. A key turning in the front door causes us to stop talking and look at the hallway. A young woman comes bounding in to the flat 'Jill' She calls down the hall hanging up her coat. She is another disgustingly cheerful morning person as she has a smile that positively glows from her face. She walks in and straight in to Jill's embrace and a good morning kiss. I am cool and nothing shows on my face.

'Good Morning Inspector, Father Steel.' She smiles in greeting but their arms are loathe to let go until Jill gets another coffee.

'Morning Sandy, How are things at the Royal Infirmary?' DI White is speaking with his mouth still working the bacon round his teeth. He obviously knew that Sandy was a girl and never let on to me. What did he expect? Tutting and disapproval? So twentieth

Century and passé obviously.

'Bloody bedlam. I have nurses nearly hysterical at the graveyard slasher. Can you not catch him or something? It is a madhouse with girls calling in sick instead of doing their shifts. Bad enough that there is a shortage of doctors but nurse numbers are critical anyway.' She's shaking her head about a subject that must rankle each and every day. Her frown is a deep one liner. Apart from that she is pretty.

'Father Andrew is helping with the case and we are hopeful.' DI white brings me in to the conversation with a nice segway. I nod without giving much away as my mouth is full of coffee.

'Well I hope you catch him quick. Are you some psychologist or profiler Father Andrew?' Her eyes narrow just a little; maybe she has had a less than satisfactory encounter with a Priest or a psychologist. The line is still there, and probably a little deeper.

'Something like that.' I smile, taking the sting out of my words and add 'I hope we can get the bastard soon.' I swig my coffee again, for emphasis.

'Well getting pissed and hungover isn't a great start to catching the bastard is it?' She laughs at our discomfort and wraps an arm around Jill's shoulders.

Their happiness evident in their ease together. Love is love, as I want everyone to accept.

'I suppose not but it was supposed to be a pint; not ten pints.' I shove DI white playfully, making him, almost, slop his coffee. I manage to stand without a groan and make my goodbyes. I need a shower and a shave and well, you know the rest. DI White is a little bit away from being ready to move so I will have time to think on my walk back to the barracks.

Chapter 21

There's a note on my door, a pink post it seriously, and it is from Father Jeremy. I peel it off and decipher his perfect handwriting. He wants me to call him the moment I get back. I wonder if that means his tipsy research last night brought some joy. I decide that my shower is much more important if I want to function properly. The walk back through the Meadows part of Edinburgh has cleared my head letting me think about the Demon. Would it really try to finish in the Cathedral? Wouldn't the consecration make it impossible for it? Perhaps because the Cathedral is open as a tourist attraction that could lessen its power over evil? I had lots of maybe type questions.

Jeremy it seems couldn't wait and, standing in my underpants, my phone rings. It is the bold Jeremy. I sigh as I answer 'Steel.' I sound tired not pissy for once. Jeremy is a bit breathy as he launches straight in with his news.

'The Cathedral is very likely. It has been done before and Basomel was the culprit.' I am pleased we know and shocked at the gall of the beast, in equal measure. Jeremy pauses for effect, or maybe it was the dun dun dun music.

'How sure are you? Last night you were only a little bit convinced.' I hate to rain on his parade but I am freezing my bollocks off here. I climb into bed to keep warm.

'Almost certain Andrew. It would be too coincidental to be an accident. I have redrawn lines on the map based on activity and project where he might have committed crimes. We are missing one but the lines cross very close to St Giles. We need to contact Bishop Michael.' He ends with a flourish or maybe it was a ta-da.

'I agree, you need to contact the Bishop.' I can hear his questioning voice now 'How sure are we? What about the police and how can we be sure? What about the public? Discretion is paramount.' I think Jeremy will be best placed to answer those directly while I have a shower. Bishop Michael would phone me right after Jeremy's call ended.

I was shaved, showered and dressed in uniform waiting for the call. The coffee I had made myself was almost gone when my phone sprang to life, Bishop Michael.

'Good Morning Bishop.' I greet him as if I am a happy morning person. It is a total change from my usual grumpy flat 'Steel' and catches him off guard. I hear the little pause and I smile to myself; I know it is childish but the small pleasures are the best.

'Good morning Andrew. I have just had a call from Father Jeremy who thinks that we have a location for tonight's denouement.' I didn't expect him to say climax.

'He believes so Bishop. I am not entirely convinced.' I let my doubts out so that if it goes wrong then I am not left holding the bag. An alibi for the future as it were.

'He seems very sure after consulting his books and historical events. I think, unless you turn up something better today, we go with the St Giles Plan.' He concludes, his tea cup clinking as he put it down.

'Plan?' It was out before I could stop it. What plan? We had a tenuous location and now there is a plan. Not a Jeremy plan please.

'Jeremy thinks we should stake it out and between you manage to dispel it. Salt and water are the best weapons he assures me, for this one.' Bishop Michael is a big picture, broad sweeps kind of bloke and this plan has more holes than cheese. I snort derisively.

'I will work on the details with Jeremy during the day Bishop.' With help from friends like these I don't fancy my chances. Fucks sake.

'As for yesterday's fiasco, I think we have that story contained.' Bishop Michael isn't finished with me yet. I probably shouldn't have snorted but you couldn't make it up. He wanted to rein me back in a bit.

'How did you manage that Bishop?' I decided to ask rather than fence with him. After all this had gone on longer than most of our phone calls and I wasn't in the mood to set a new world record for pointless conversations with your boss.

'The Home Secretary got a film director to say it was a reaction test for his next movie that might be set in Edinburgh. Secret cameras were following the action and all that. It was a stunt with actors, he was on the BBC last night doing the piece.' I am supposed to be in awe, obviously.

'That should play well with the footage that will be all over the internet from the phones. Hopefully everyone buys it. I need to go Bishop was there anything else?' I need to get a hold of Jeremy, maybe literally, and retrain him on how I do things.

'Nothing more Andrew. I will be back at the residence tomorrow afternoon, we can catch up once this little problem is resolved. Be careful Andrew and discrete if you can.'

'I will Bishop.' I make a face like a teenager. I am back to my usual sour expression as I end the call. Fuck. Fuck. Fuck.

I phone Jeremy while I am still irritated and I am even more so as I get his voicemail, not a great start but I leave him the call me message with no hint of my desire to rip his head off. Plan? He has absolutely no idea. He will have us waiting outside in Spanish Inquisition robes or hiding round the corner waiting like the keystone cops. I have two zip-lock bags full of Dead Sea salt and six little crystal vials of Holy water lying out on my bed as I check my weaponry. I have a little jar of Chrism, which I sniff, I love the balsam smell. I always feel better afterwards.

'Jeremy.' I answer the buzzing phone without swearing which seemed a racing certainty just a moment or two ago. I wonder what he will say his cunning plan comprises of.

'I have spoken to Bishop Michael and he thinks we should presume that St Giles will be the location of the event tonight.' He pauses for effect, to which I don't respond. 'We should get DI White to stake out the Cathedral and we should be ready nearby.' He pauses for breath.

'I think we need to go to the incident room and talk to the Chief Superintendent and explain your great plan.' I wonder if my finely tuned sarcasm has reached him. His next comment proves that he is immune or stupid.

'I think you are right, we will need his permission and resources. I will meet you there. I will leave now.' He seems a little excited and that might just get him killed and if that happens I, probably, will be likely to join him. If I get him killed then the Bishop won't be best pleased. Life is so unfair.

I will be a while before I get there to sort out his mess. I have an appointment with the Father Confessor.

Chapter 22

I dislike Confession, or Penance as we should call it these days. I bet that I am not alone. Over a billion Catholics worldwide probably dislike it just as much as I do but I know that if I am to fight on the Lord's behalf tonight I need to do it with a soul cleaner than a brand new Kleenex. Any little chink of sin or darkness lingering about me will make me vulnerable. The need for purity is not one I used to consider all that important but I figure that it certainly might keep me alive tonight. Afraid? Me? Probably.

My enemy has a name and centuries of form at this sort of thing and what do I have? Father Jeremy of the dusty old tomes and some salt. Seems like a fair fight is in the offing although I still can't see that we can destroy the Demon. Drive him off, maybe but destroy? I think we will need more than salt, water and Faith. A flame thrower might be a more appropriate weapon or maybe a more effective one.

I am a little early and I can feel the serenity of the

chapel as the late Autumn sun slants through the windows. Although it is a modern building of low quality seventies build, the feeling of peace in this place always works for me. I can really descend into the inner place that prayer facilitates after the 'God bless Mummy, God bless Daddy' are past and real worship begins. I am sarcastic, caustic even, but when I give thanks and beg forgiveness I feel the emptiness of my soul and it is a humbling place. It is then that I know what hell would be.

The tinkling of a little bell telling me that the Father Confessor is in and my sacrament of Penance is about to begin. I move to the booth, letting everything temporal fall away and the need for spiritual cleansing is all I focus on. I pull the curtain closed and hear the slot slide back as I sit in the near dark of the confessional booth.

'In the name of the Father, the Son and the Holy Spirit. Amen.' His deep rumbling voice fills my ears. Now it is my turn to begin.

'Bless me Father for I have sinned. It has been some time since my last confession. I am a sinner who does the work of the lord and my weaknesses and frailties are many and manifest.' I begin, slightly formal but I always feel that my words are heard by the Holy Father so I try not to be informal.

The Confessional Seal is just that, sealed and the sins I beg forgiveness for range a cross a wide range of small medium and large. The problem I have is that I know I will probably commit them all again and again and my contrition is suspect at best. I suppose I am contrite and would in an ideal world retire to the scholarly pursuits that the wonderful libraries could offer but I am the sword in the hand of the Lord and I know that in the progress of swinging that sword I wander through a trough of sin and I add to it frequently.

The Father Confessor is listening intently to my words and I have frequent pauses to gather my thoughts, he doesn't do much more than encourage me to find the root cause of my behaviour. It is hard questioning and he has no idea what I actually do here and why I am so problematic and self destructive. I feel totally wrung out at the end of our session and I think he realises that there is little left uncovered and unexamined.

'My Son, go and make your peace with Our Lord. Your sins I absolve but you need to absolve yourself and let the grace of the Lord flourish within you. Stop fighting his plan for you and accept. Go in peace to love and serve the Lord in the Name of the Father, The Son and The Holy Spirit, Amen.' The words the final act in our conversation. From my lips to God's ear indeed and his encouragement is exactly what I need. I return to the pew and reconnect myself with why I am what I am and who I am working for.

By two thirty I am in the incident room drinking tea and waiting on DI White to get off the phone. PC Jill has looked after me while I had to wait. Of Father Jeremy there is no sign at the moment and, for that at least, I am glad. The walls of pictures and notes tell us the square root of heehaw and I feel sorry for my colleagues in the blue uniforms. This was a crime series they could never solve and never protect the populace from. Some things just don't fit in the tick box forms as to why a case remains unsolved.

DI White puts the phone down and waves me in, he is smiling a little. Is he punch drunk or pleased to see me? I smile back and sit in the soft seat opposite his desk and watch him swill down , what I presume is, sludge in the bottom of his cup.

'I have the Chief Super's permission to set up a

perimeter of uniformed officers in the area, discretely, and a flying squad to make the swoop.' He pauses expectantly and carries on as I nod. 'The plan is a simple stake out and wait. If Chummy arrives with a victim we pounce and effect an arrest.'

'An Arrest? Seriously? We will have to banish the bastard. There won't be an arrest.' For Fucks sake. I had such high hopes for DI White too. It seems his police training is very hard to overcome.

'Well I suppose not. We need to stop it from taking any more lives and as you say banish it. Father Jeremy wondered if It would take over another body for tonight.' DI White was a little embarrassed at his back sliding, for which I forgive him.

'I am not convinced that it will show up at the Cathedral. Father Jeremy is working on slim pickings in terms of clues. Logically it sounds fine and meets the expected behaviours but I am just not sure. We need to be able to move if it turns out to be a bust.' I am frowning, I can feel it.

'How many men do we have to brief? Obviously the Home Office want this kept quiet. What shall we tell them?' I am thinking out loud and trying not to put problems in front of us but we need to plan better than the fag-packet plan that we currently have on the table.

'I can keep it down to a small reliable core who will keep their mouths shut but you will need to do it. They will think I am just winding them up.' DI White looks longingly at his cup of sludge, probably jealous of my fresh hot cup.

'Four will be enough the rest will be on crowd control duty, stopping it getting out but they probably won't see anything. We can do a wash up and debrief at the end before anyone leaves for the night.' I try to sound like I am an old hand at this. I wonder if DI White is buying in to the image.

'Okay four it will be. Jill, MacBride, Murdoch and Anderson. They are all reliable and my team.' I nod, I think he knows his people better than anyone.

'Perhaps a proper briefing including the Chief Super will be a good idea. Where is Jeremy?' I want to get things ready and then get a little sleep before tonight's main event. Although at this time of year it will be dark soon so night is a long time in Scotland. The streets will be dark and shadowy soon allowing the enemy a little bit of cover and an opportunity to carry out his plan.

'No idea. He said he needed to get some provisions for tonight. He was pretty vague, if you know what I mean.' White's shrug speaks volumes. He doesn't understand Jezza either.

The phone on the desk springs into a fit of violent ringing and gets snatched up as a self defence mechanism. 'DI White, how can I help you?' He is such a professional. A quick conversation with a few 'yes sir's thrown in tell me it is the brass upstairs. It is a mercifully short call.

'We are wanted upstairs. The Chief Constable wants a word with us. It seems the Chief Super isn't happy about our progress and didn't like the lack of detail about the case.' DI White straightens his tie, trying to look less crumpled than usual. I am in uniform, a fact that is guaranteed to get me the respect I need. Probably not.

'While I understand your frustration gentlemen, the Home Secretary has made my presence here a need to know and I am unable to go much further at this time. We will have a resolution tonight, that is all I can tell you at this point.' I am reasonableness incarnate and playing like an adult. Two things that happen only very infrequently. Must remember to write it in my diary.

'Dammit man, I am the Chief Constable. If I want an answer I will have one. There will be no use of my men and resources until I know what is going on in my own force.' He has gotten a little bit purple at the refusal, however polite.

'No one is more aware of that than I am, Sir. If it would help you could call Bishop Michael or the Home Secretary and ask them to give me dispensation to break the Official Secrets Act.' I was pushing it a bit. I could just tell them but his attitude pissed me off. He was one of the 'Do you know who I am?' brigade and they get as little as I can give them. His spluttering at my use of the Home Secretary is warming; good to know my trump card still has its uses.

'I am not happy Father Steel. There are bodies filling up our morgue and no sign of a collar. And now you tell me it will be resolved tonight. I am sorry if I sound sceptical but I have a responsibility to the people of Edinburgh and this need to know is frankly not acceptable.' The purple is fading and now he wants to be reasonable. I decide that these two might as well get the talk, there is no way forward without it. I look like I am wrestling for a moment on the horns of a dilemma before looking at them in turn.

'Very well Chief Constable. I will, of course, need to pass on the details of this conversation to the Home Office but I will tell you what I can.' I look him square in the eye. He nods accepting my threat and I can see a little triumphant gleam in his eye. He has banged his desk and gotten his own way. 'I am empowered by the State and the Churches to investigate all matters that are supernatural in origin. This case is one such matter.' I put my hand up to stop the blustering interruption that is forming on his lips.

'You have a demon stalking the streets of Edinburgh. Why it is here, who summoned it and many other questions are unanswered but we know where it will be tonight. When we catch it, I will destroy it and there will be no more killings from this one.' I say everything gently but with a 'you asked' underneath.

'That is ridiculous.' The Chief Constable lets it out. He thinks I am now just pissing him about. He leans forward all lurking body mass and thinks that will intimidate me.

'Ridiculous or not it is true. My credentials and authority are before you. I am sure you could have them checked out again if you are uncertain. This demon has been a busy boy and we are on the verge of resolving the issue. I am sure that is paramount in this matter is it not?' I hold his gaze with mine. I could have said 'Do as you are fucking told' but that apparently isn't in the play nice section.

'A fucking Demon.' He is struggling with the concept. Well, I suppose it does sound unreasonable to the Head Plod. I'd bet he came through uniform or traffic; never had an original thought in his life I expect.

'Yes a fucking Demon, with whom I have been up close and personal three times now. We will be able to finish the job tonight and that will be the end of the matter. The stunt out of the Dungeon was the Demon and it took some covering up.' He looks at DI White, looking for him to refute my claim and doesn't get one.

'Fuck.' There we go, he seems to be catching up as he flops back into his high-backed leather executive chair.

I look at him and let a little hint of a grin grow on my face 'Exactly Chief Constable.' It seems we are on the same page now.

I look to the Chief Superintendent and he is a little pale. He might need his hand held. I doubt the advanced leaders course prepared him for this kind of thing, he might need to man up.

Chapter 23

'That was fun.' DI White is smirking all the way back to the incident room. I try not to encourage him but the cheeky grin just won't stay off my face. The Chief Constable was very accommodating and didn't need to call the Home Secretary once he was on the right page. The page that said Demon running amok. I don't think the Chief Superintendent is going to recover quite that quickly. Especially after my dire warnings about losing his pension and suffering possible prosecution. I'd bet they are having a little fortification in the Chief Constable's office, they both need it; poor things.

'Well they did force me to tell them. So I am totally blameless on this one. They didn't babble too much did they?' DI White and I are at the elevator waiting for the doors to open when I hear a breathy foot slapping approach, Father Jeremy has caught up with us. He seems all agitated and will need to be calmed down.

'Jeremy, lovely to see you.' The words and tone

sound reasonable but the inner dialogue is less charitable and probably just reeks of irritation.

'Father Andrew, Inspector.' He nods as he pulls oxygen into his lungs. It appears the silly sod may have just run up the stairs in time to go back down in the lift. 'I have been reading and have a suggestion for tonight.' He is about to launch into an explanation right here, in public waiting on the lift.

'Jeremy' I cut across him a little abruptly perhaps, 'We can cover that in the incident room.' The fact that I had to tell him was irritating enough but the fact that his discretion bypass had kicked in meant he hadn't thought about the consequences of his blabbing mouth. I am glad he doesn't take Confession, he would be hopeless at keeping it private.

He is bursting to tell me something and the whole three minutes until we are back in DI White's office must have felt like an eternity to him. I shut the door and almost get my arse into a seat when Jeremy draws a breath to expound his pearl of wisdom.

'Salt.' Obviously the looks on our faces make it clear that we understand totally and he continues 'Basomel cannot tolerate salt.' Well that cleared everything up. Or rather it didn't.

'And?' I need to prompt him because if I don't he will stand there like we should applaud his amazing three point shot. Although I doubt he has any idea what a three point shot actually is.

'We should cross each threshold with salt leaving only one for him to pass over and then we should pounce.' I wonder if he has been imbibing but maybe he is just a bit mental.

'Would that work?' DI White asks, he hasn't learned yet to not encourage Jeremy but I expect he will learn soon. Religious scholars are great at advice, plans and theoretical ways that should work but usually they fall apart in the crucible of doing.

'No.' I butt in but Jezza is on a roll.

'Yes, theoretically. If Basomel cannot pass the salt then we can contain him.' He sounds so sure.

'Tell me about that pouncing thing?' I wonder if he realises that I speak sarcasm like he speaks English. I must be bilingual. The stunned look on his face has just unearthed the bit of his theoreticals that he hasn't gotten to yet.

'Well, I , well....I thought that would be your bit.' He stammered along wilting under my direct gaze.

'How do we banish him Jeremy?' I think I need to

know if I need a ritual or just to beat him to death with salt and holy water. So far he hasn't really been much help on this front.

'Well, as I said, he cannot tolerate salt so we would need to use salt as our main weapon.' He is fumbling along, searching for a lifeboat.

'The salt will be fine for driving him where we want him to go. I am just a bit concerned that once I am between him and escape what I can do to stop him. He is a powerful foe and just winging it will get us all killed. Or at least some of us.' I have my, now legendary, scowl settled on my face.

'You have your faith and the salt should be enough.' The sanctimonious prick has that look on his superior face that makes me feel like slapping him until my hands can't do it any more.

'Where do we come in?' DI White is looking for sensible instruction, he has obviously come to the wrong place.

'You will need to pull the victim to safety and then seal me in with the salt. You know Thunderdome style.' They both look at me like I am talking in tongues.

'Fucks sake! Mad Max three, Thunderdome? Two

men enter one man leave.' I shake my head, what a pair of cultural pygmies. Who can forget Auntie in that chain mail vest?

'You will need to keep it from getting out. No matter what, if it cannot finish the ritual by midnight then it will return to its place. If it completes the ritual something bad will definitely happen. We don't want that now do we?' I am in full sarky-bastard mode.

'We still do not know exactly what the culmination of its ritual will herald. It is very difficult to know what the outcome could be.' Jeremy has returned to saying he has been able to find out very little that is of any real use.

'Sealing the Cathedral with salt is actually a decent shout but we can't do that until it is inside; otherwise he will know it is a trap.' I had to grudgingly accept that the salt trap sealing the entrances and windows might just be a good idea.

'So you need to be inside waiting then?' DI white has picked up on the crap bit of the plan. Or at least it is the crap bit as far as I am concerned. Wait inside a Cathedral for a seven foot plus black and red skinned, fanged, clawed demon who wants to rape and eviscerate a human sacrifice to complete a ritual.

Why wouldn't I be happy to be the one waiting to interrupt its coitus with a stinging shower of salt? Maybe I just need to lighten up.

'That sounds dangerous. I will wait with you.' DI White drops his bombshell like facing almost certain death and imperilling his mortal soul is nothing. It is the most amazing gift to his fellow man a man could give.

'I think you need to be outside controlling things and making sure nothing goes wrong.' I try to put him off but I am so proud of him. I hope the moistening and tightening around my eyes doesn't let a tear escape.

'It'll be fine. I will be inside, on the scene and I have deputies for dealing with the outside. The matter is settled.' DI White is a great human being. Obviously mental but great nonetheless.

'Okay then but we will need a few rules.'

The four of them were sitting there in the interview room, waiting. The banter was flowing when DI White and I strolled in. The tables were impromptu seats as they looked at us, wondering what needed privacy. Wasn't the incident room private enough? Of the four, three I knew and had seen about the place the fourth must be Anderson. He was from vice or cyber protection and had come up with DI White. He could be trusted, apparently.

'Okay settle down. This won't take long.' DI White interrupted the back and forth piss taking that was still flowing and I think MacBride was losing badly. He was taking it well though. 'Father Steel needs to brief you for tonight's operation.'

'Thanks. Tonight will see the end of our operation but I need to brief you on a few salient, if unusual points before we start. What you are about to hear is covered by the Official Secrets Act and doesn't leave this room. It will mean much more than pensions and careers. It will be a closed court and indefinite detainment.' I pause looking at the blood drained faces. This they did not expect. I smile gently before adding 'So far it hasn't come to that. You have been chosen by DI White as people I can trust and rely upon. So I am about to share secrets that are difficult to accept on first hearing but believe me when I say every word is fact.' I pause again, the imperceptible nods of agreement ripple through them, with a few glances to DI White who is ignoring them and focussed intently on my delivery.

'I work for the Home Office and the Church and whenever a crime against the Church takes place I am called to take a look. I only deal with cases involving supernatural events. These murders are one such event.' I wait for the disbelief in the supernatural to show on their faces but there is nothing so I soldier on. Murdoch doesn't even have his heard it all now look on.

'The murderer is a Demon summoned to complete a ritual tonight by Midnight.' I stop and look at them. Anderson flashes a look at DI White which may have had a subtext of 'Thanks mate, thanks a lot' or something like it.

'How do we fight a Demon?' MacBride is in first bless him. I like practical but for my first group briefing I had hoped for a little more awe and much more babbling. Neither of which seems to be forthcoming.

'You don't. I do. I have certain advantages and abilities for this sort of thing. Although fighting Demons is anything but straight forward.' I smile a little by wryly. Usually after fighting Demons I have a long rest courtesy of the National Health Service.

'What do we need to do?' Murdoch's deep voice

rumbles out past the moustache and the others look at me, expectantly.

'I will be inside with DI White and you, with many other officers will be outside. DI Anderson will be a proxy for DI White and will run the plays. The other officers will know nothing but will need corralled when things kick off. You will make sure that the others do as they are ordered and keep them away from seeing anything sensitive. We need to know that outside the Cathedral we have people who know what is going on and will follow the plan.'

They all look suitably sober and contemplative and I wonder if religious observance plays any part in their lives. Well maybe it will in the future. Jill is a church goer but that might be out of habit or an attempt to lay the ground work to marry her girlfriend.

'One more thing, Father Jeremy will be outside with you. He may be able to give important information if things go in an unplanned direction.' I can't believe that I just told them to ask Jeremy if things go wrong. Although if things go as wrong as they might then DI White and I won't care. We'll be dead.

Chapter 24

We have adjourned to eat and rest, now that the planning is done. DI White has a big team and our specialists. Over thirty officers will be in holding patterns nearby and a few will be working near the Cathedral to make sure that Jeremy can seal the box, as it were. He seems to have decided that we only need to seal portals and not every window, and there are lots of them. I hope he is right about that. I don't want it flying through a window and off up, or down, the Royal Mile. I doubt we could use the same hush story a second time.

I have had a Big Mac and fries on the way back to the Seminary, a very modern last meal if ever there was one. I nearly had the Quarter Pounder with cheese but decided to push the boat out. Anyway on the way back to my room I have been thinking about a weapon. Something I can use on Basomel if he gets a bit frisky or close. Or Both. I decide to phone Jeremy and see if he has any suggestions that might work but his Faith answer earlier doesn't really fill me with hope.

'Jeremy, I need a weapon for tonight. Any suggestions?' I miss out the introductions and foreplay getting straight to the nitty-gritty. I can almost see his eyebrows dancing up into his hairline.

'A weapon?' He seems to forget that I will be up close and personal while he will be outside surrounded by policemen.

'Yes a weapon. Something to fend him off with if he gets too close. Do we have any sacred daggers or anything?' I have seen loads of films where the hero has a special weapon to defeat the enemy. A sword would be better; well bigger anyway.

'No we don't but salt will hurt him while you do the rite of banishment.' He seems not to get it.

'And while I am ploughing through the words what is to stop Basomel ripping my throat out?' It has obviously been on my mind all day. I await a pearl of wisdom to flow from his lips. I might have to wait a while.

'The salt should bind him to the earth and you can always scald with scripture.' I am sure he believes that. However, when a large fanged and taloned demon is coming towards you with an unhappy look in its eye reciting scripture gets a little tricky.

'Thanks Jeremy, thanks a lot.' I hang up and think about possible weapons that might work for me.

After an hour of snooping about I have found a whip. I am not really all that sure how to use it but if I soak it in Dead Sea salt then maybe it will work. There was a set of darts sticking in the common room board but I didn't think they would be up to much. I also considered a sock with a couple of pool balls and salt as a sort of club but I ruled that out too.

I set to prepping the whip and try to get it as wet and salty as I can. I am pretty pleased with the result and I think I am on to something here. My new found idea will need to be run past the Bishop if tonight goes well. A patent to follow, perhaps.

I practice a few sweeps and realise it is all in the wrist. The swish and snap is pretty loud and it appears I am a natural whip wielder. Maybe all those hours watching Indiana Jones at the cinema have paid off. I am getting there in terms of hitting my door, every time from about nine feet. Armed now I can set to learning the ritual that I might need to recite by heart. I need to know the structure of the Abjuration and Dismissal, any set out of sequence might allow Basomel to escape the utter destruction he so fully deserves.

The time is marching on and after a period of reflection as I prayed, I am ready. The police car waiting for me at the seminary steps is like a prom night Limousine, ready to carry me off to a place I have never been; deliberately locked in a Cathedral with a Demon. I will need to add that to my CV and highlights reel.

DI White is briefing the troops and while very efficient and police speak; it has nothing on my secret briefing earlier today. The glances from Jill, Murdoch, MacBride and Anderson are knowing and somewhat terrified. I smile back trying to give them a level of assurance that all will be fine not exactly what I am feeling inside. The positioning and call signs are allocated and the hands for questions are going up.

DI White is covering them with his full police Inspector training. He is using his professional, no nonsense voice that is totally at odds with his slightly crumpled outfit.

I wonder that his wife lets him out like that and find myself wondering if he is divorced like so many of the senior policemen are these days. It seems to have a high attrition rate and I suppose I shouldn't be surprised that the hours take their toll. I suppose that it is hard to go home to normal things after looking at a body stuffed in a bin. I know he has kids, he mentioned them a few times, Kevin, I think, and Alison. A little weary light came into his eyes when they came up in conversation, teenagers I think.

'Father Steel and I will be based in the Cathedral, we expect chummy to turn up there.' I am pulled back to the now by the saying of my name. It is funny how we always seem to pick our names out of any room full of conversation; a bit like a radio scanner, locking on at a few syllables. A few heads turn in my direction and I try not to flush at the attention, it's not like I can help it. I am rescued by the entry of the Chief Constable, can't remember his name, and the standing to attention of everyone in the room.

'Carry on Detective Inspector.' He stands to one side with the Chief Superintendent following him like a house elf. I smirk at the idea of Dobbie following the Chief Constable.

I notice everyone sitting just a bit straighter in their seats and eyes a bit more focussed on every word of DI White and not a smart arsed comment forthcoming. They are all so professional and taking instruction from the Gold Commander, DI White, and making sure they understand what is expected. The Sergeants are now detailing the pairs and vehicles and expected station points and confirming call signs.

The Chief is making sure that DI White has this under control and has just informed him of something unpleasant, or at least going by the clenching of the jaw. I wander over, a spare prick at this wedding for now. The Chief tries not to glower in my direction as I approach.

'Gentlemen.' As if I should be included, I don't need to draw my hall pass do I? They look at me together but no one wants to say 'piss off' so I wait like a bad smell. They will need to continue.

'Chief Superintendent Saunderson will be in the control room managing communications and despatch options.' The Chief wants his flunky in control and DI White most certainly doesn't. Neither do I but I doubt it will make a difference as we will do what we need to anyway.

'Have you thought about managing any story leakage? Any plans for preventative messaging to prevent the online spreading of police concentration in that area?' I fire this in just to be an awkward sod, seems that they haven't even thought of that. That will give them something to do while DI White and I get ourselves sorted out. I lead him into the office where his piles of paperwork are almost like a chaotic work of art.

'You need to be protected so I have a few things for you. Firstly this.' I hand him a bag with salt in it. He is impressed, I can tell. 'It is Dead Sea Salt and if the Demon ever gets its hands on you throw it in its face and run for it. Although if it gets to you that means it already has gotten to me and we are truly in the shit.' I smile in a way that is meant to be funny but he isn't all that sure. I hand him two vials of holy water.

'Use these as a spray or as a grenade. Same as the salt, if you need them we're fucked.' I laugh and he joins in. Good lad. It is like demon fighting kit for beginners and I am not sure that they will help that much.

'Finally, I will bless you and mark you for God. Are you baptised?' He nods again, weighing up the salt and water combination I have given him. I pull my jar of Chrism from my pocket at taking a tiny fingerprint worth stand before him.

'The Blessings of God the Father, God the Son and God the Holy Spirit be upon you. With this unction I mark you as one of God's flock. His Love within you, His protection around you. Amen.' I mark a cross on his forehead, leaving a little shiny cross that no one will notice. If they do they will take the pure piss out of him, colleagues can be so cruel.

Father Jeremy has the job of organising the sealing of the Cathedral, he will be meeting us there with enough salt to do the job. I wonder if road grit would do the job? Probably not. Salt as always been a tool of the Lord, ever since he turned Lot's wife into a pillar of it at Sodom. She watches over the Dead Sea allegedly. Who am I to argue?

We agree that we will be in position from nine o'clock making sure that we don't miss Basomel and allow him to complete his mission. The victim will still be alive when he gets to the Cathedral. The tricky bit will be separating him from her and making sure he can't consummate the act that will bring the, proverbial, roof down. If we get the timing wrong then we will be the dessert. The power that will flood through him will make him almost indestructible and our little tools will do little against him. I worry about the nullification of the consecrated ground of the Cathedral, if Basomel can pull that off again the game will be, well and truly, a bogey.

'Have you done this before?' DI White asks as he drives the unmarked police car through the streets of the Old Town. I wonder which this' he means and decide I'd better answer the one I think he means, you know, the Demon slaying.

'Yes. I have dealt with a demon before. They are vicious and dangerous so don't get in its way.' I look across at him and realise I don't want anything to happen to him; he is one of the good guys. I'd better keep him safe.

'That's good to know. I'd hate to think I volunteered with a beginner.' He smirks, humour being the best antidote for fear.

'The last one left me in hospital for a while but you should have seen the mess of him.' The laughs fill the car, not that it was that funny but the need to let it out and embrace the lunacy of waiting in a Cathedral at night for a horny, psychotic demon to turn up with a victim and interrupt it.

Chapter 25

The Royal Mile is still a busy place at nine o'clock on a Sunday night; revellers, students and tourists enjoying the bars and restaurants that are numerous on both sides of the cobbled streets. The grey stones shine, slick with moisture from the drizzle, giving the street a magical look. The overhead street decorations of fluorescent reds and greens bringing a smile to lots of faces. Don't they know about the murders? Probably not, they all seem to live with such a relish of life that I am a little jealous. Was I ever happy? When did life stop being a good place if it ever was? Buggered if I know.

We pass a couple of marked cars that don't look out of place in the street. The fact that the weather isn't great should see most of the possible witnesses inside and not in the street, although going by the shortness of skirts the local girls don't feel the cold. Their clothes more suitable for the balmy summer evenings not the late Autumn ones where cold is in fact an overstatement. Scotland's weather is the single biggest contributor to the miserable bastard syndrome that infests the totality of the male population, that and the performance of the national football team.

Luckily the women are not so infested. DI White parks in the City Chambers reserved parking, as if he cares that it states permit holders only, The buff sandstone arches look really grand as you drive under them and on to the cobbles where the Lord Provost of Edinburgh parks his car. The building is beautiful too, if you like architecture. Location is everything, City Chambers next to the Cathedral, next to the Courts of Session and just downhill from a castle.

We make our way across the street to the Cathedral and along the long wall, the main entrance is facing the castle, we pass the old side doors and a busker has set up his pitch there. He is giving it all he has with John Lennon's Imagine, and I am sure he will be arrested for the assault he is committing on a great song. His caterwaul has attracted a few umbrella wielding spectators. They seem impervious to the low quality delivery and even part with a few coins. Maybe they feel sorry for him.

'He's not one of ours is he?' I nudge my partner,

laughing at his 'Fuck no' response. We turn the corner and stop to spit on the cobbles. The mosaic of the Heart of Midlothian sits on the site of the old prison, cheek by jowl with the courts and the church. It is tradition to spit on it although I suspect the Hibee fans really enjoy giving it some gob. In Edinburgh we have two football teams Hearts and Hibs; although I don't care about the pointless beautiful game, I know that the undercurrent of religious sectarianism makes their rivalry ugly. Not quite as ugly as the soap dodgers from Glasgow rivalry between Celtic and Rangers. Still it exists in the capital.

Jeremy is standing in the rain like a plonker, if he had waited in the lee of the arch he would have been dry; maybe he likes to be miserable. He waves as we approach, it doesn't look too out of place, after all priests wave at each other all the time. Just not like a hysterical lunatic.

I wave back in a decorous for-fucks-sake-stop-being-an-arse kind of way. DI White nods and tries not to encourage him, I wish I had thought of that. In no time at all Father Jeremy is ushering us inside like we didn't know the way. I have been in this Cathedral many times and I doubt it is new to DI White either.

Jeremy is getting all excited and breathless, again. Heaven help us.

'There are four possible entrances and only the front door will be open. When he arrives we will be waiting ready to seal the entrances. Jill has the back, Murdoch and MacBride have the other two. DI Anderson and I will seal the main doors.' Obviously Father Jeremy and the rest will be pivotal tot he success of trapping DI White and myself inside with a demon. He had better get it right.

The inside of St Giles sits waiting like a bride waiting for her groom, so serene and silent. The feeling from the flagstones is one of centuries of penitence and piety, I can't imagine that Basomel will find it comfortable touching the stone. I look at the high stained glass panels, so intricate and lovely in their colours and symbolism. I bask a little in the whole sanctity before White coughs gently.

'Where should we wait?' He asks quietly, the reverence obviously reaching him too. I look round, I hadn't really thought about it really. I suppose the high Pulpit will be the best place; near the middle and give time for the doors to be sealed behind it. There is also a little bit of cover, making us less obvious in the first instance. The high Altar is still some way behind us, giving us an interception chance; always making the assumption that it will come through the main doors. After all it is a supremely arrogant and showy demon.

'This used to be four churches, you know.' DI White adds some local tour guide knowledge. He seems embarrassed to know something about the Church. I look at him, waiting fro him to go on. 'We did it at high school. About twenty years ago now. John Knox used to rant and rave from up there.' He waves his hand airily across the Nave.

'Four churches?' This is news to me. If that's the case would this be the place for the final sacrifice? We might be waiting here for an event that will not be happening here. I wonder if the knowledgable Jeremy knows this.

'Yeah but I can't remember the names though. One was the Old Kirk. It is the main Church of Scotland church anyway.' He isn't feeling my worry.

'It is called a Cathedral but I wonder if that is a modern affectation?' I frown, I need to know. It is old but not ancient and has been restored in the last hundred and fifty years or so.

'Jeremy. Did you know the Cathedral was four churches originally?' I speak quickly into my phone. 'It might not be the site. Would any of the other churches nearby be better options for Him? Find out quick. We don't want to be waiting about with our dicks in our hands while he does the ritual elsewhere.' Fuck.

'Go and find out.' I practically hiss at him, I know I am being unreasonable but how the hell did he not know this. Just because it is a big religious building, it doesn't make it the most likely. I can feel a chill running all over my skin. I know now we need to check the other churches nearby.

'Can you task some officers to check the other nearby ones we talked about yesterday. The Wee free one and the Tron. Tell them to look for signs of entry or anything suspicious.' I am getting a bit edgy. I stomp up to the Altar, letting the stained glass panels calm me before snatching my buzzing phone to my ear.

'It was four churches.' Jeremy starts with the obvious. I think he might be a bit upset with his own stupidity; well add him to the club. 'It was a Cathedral when it was Episcopal but has been seen as the High

Kirk since the Reformation.'

I practically snarl down the phone. 'I don't need you to read Wikipedia to me. Find out if this is the likeliest site or if we are in the wrong place.' I cut him off and shout to DI White. 'This will be the wrong place. Have you got people looking at the others?' He holds a finger up to me making me wait as I approach him. He nods as he passes instructions. My phone buzzes again.

'What?' I snap without looking at it. I really should have looked first. If I had I might have avoided upsetting the Chief Superintendent who is all concerned about the possible change of plan.

'Sorry, I thought you were someone else.' I try to row back my tetchiness but I don't think we will be on Christmas card lists this year.

'This is turning in to a bloody shambles.' I turn to DI White as we have that moment where we both know we are fucked. Individually and collectively. 'I don't mind my own fuck ups but I don't need any help.' I state, the sour look on my face would curdle milk.

Chapter 26

I have always been, what you might call, volatile. It's not as if I don't realise I am over-reacting, I do, but I just can't stop it once the fuse it lit. My mother used to tell me it would cause me problems in later life. I don't know if she meant a heart attack, stroke or just no pals. Probably meant all three. I am stomping about like an elk in the Rut and filling this hallowed Cathedral with under the breath swearwords and not so under the breath swearwords. I wonder how many fucks this Cathedral has heard over the years ; well I have added a great many and regrets I have not a single one. Father Jeremy comes in looking like a kicked puppy and he is lucky that my spleen has been well and truly vented.

'This better be good news Jeremy.' I growl as he approaches. His face is tripping him, a wonderful Scottish description for looking like he is going to cry. He stops out of punching distance which seems an unnecessary precaution.

'This is probably not the site. I have made a few

calls and the split nature of the consecrations wouldn't make it a prime site for his needs.' He is staring at a space past me, where DI White looks much more forgiving.

'Probably?' I spit, incredulity filling every fibre of my being. 'I think we need a little more than that. If we go chasing around the city centre to find the site of this cosmic event and can't find him we might all be seriously up shit creek.' I know I am being unfair but we need a little bit of definite information.

'He might still choose here as it would be suitable but just not the key prize we thought he might seek.' Jeremy is chewing the inside of his cheek like an eight year old who hasn't done their homework. Basically we have no idea and Jezza is carrying that can. It doesn't matter how many 'we' statements he slips in. Collective responsibility in action; no it will end up being my fault and I am less than happy about it.

'No sign of entry at the other two local churches.' DI White feeds back the information coming through on his radio. Well that is something I suppose; although it makes us even more clueless.

'Jeremy, we will continue with the plan for now until we know otherwise. I can't think of any older churches near here. Can you?' He shakes his head telling me what I really knew. We are well and truly in the shit, right up to our necks.

'Call the Bishop or someone who can help and find out where the nearest churches are by age. DI White and I will wait in here. Who knows maybe Basomel is as utterly clueless as to the history of this Cathedral as we were.' I flop down into a pew and look to the high altar for some divine inspiration.

DI White sits on the other side of the aisle and fiddles with his phone; texting someone. I want to be angry but I feel it all slipping away as the loss begins to strike home. It looks like we will lose this one. I don't actually know what the hell I am actually trying to prevent, I just know it would be bad. I look a my watch, it helpfully reads cowboy time; ten to ten. I smile as the tune of bonanza plays in my head. It is the smile of the desperate, I need something to go right tonight and so far it has been a series of cock-ups.

I laugh and it startles DI White from his smartphone and it turns out he was playing candycrush and not texting. He looks guilty thinking that his playing was the cause of my mirth. 'It could be worse you know? We could have been sealed in here with a Demon.' I grin and he grins back. Two clowns laughing in the face of adversity, so very British..

'You were a little hard on Father Jeremy. He might just have saved both our lives by being useless.' DI White leans back and stretches, tension has made him stiff and tense.

'Probably. It will cost someone else theirs though. Our good fortune has a price, one neither of us wants to pay.' I go from cheeky grin to morose bastard in nano-seconds, another wonderful trait inherited I am sure. 'I need to pray. You just amuse yourself and don't let us get sneaked up on.' I wink to tell him I am joking.

I need to think and the act of kneeling with my eyes closed and letting my mind de-clutter itself is the way I know best. Everyone would assume I am praying but it is more a mental exercise of clearing all the crap from my mind and letting the solution to my pressing issues come to the surface. I let my mind drift away from this here and now and try to feel my way around the four churches I am knelling upon. It feels holy but a bit messy, like the energy is confused and basically an ineffective barrier to the powers of the Dark. I wonder who did the consecration; Presbyterians are a bit different and lack much of a ritual to call the power of God to sanctify the whole of this lovely building.

The power of prayer to invoke the almighty is a powerful tool and I am sure that as the masses took part in the service of consecration there was a great deal of power laid down and tying in the essence of the Hermit Saint Giles. I begin to pray in earnest hoping that my words fly straight to the ears of the Almighty and that he deigns to listen to me and give me some sort of answer. Of course, he doesn't usually reply and I certainly won't be holding my breath waiting on a direct response. It isn't like a hotline although it would be handy if there was one.

'Hi God, Sorry to bother you but Jeremy has made an arse of this; can you just give me a clue. Not even a big one. Just a clue or pointer to get us moving in the right direction. Thanks. Much appreciated.' I play this ridiculous musing in my head as my inner voice wanders like an irreverent teenager that thinks it is funny and it patently isn't.

I let myself slip into an open kind of state. I don't know what to do nor what to expect. Divine inspiration is a bit tricky to predict and accounts for the Stigmatics and the ecstatics and the collapsing in tongues brigade. I am lucky that my symptoms are a little more normal and not the most extreme end. After all bleeding hands and feet must be very inconvenient and unnerving. My breathing slows and I can feel the lightness that may be my meditative state or the lack of oxygen to my synapses. I wait.

The wash of power flowing towards me seems to emanate from the west, it is like a ripple on a still pond of psychic energy. Like someone dropped a bloody big boulder into a deep still pool. The shudder that passes through me brings me back to the here and now. My eyes flash open like the spooky fright bit from a horror film. DI White jumps like a big Jessie, he was staring at me apparently. How long he has been waiting for me to come round I have no idea.

'Father, it is ten past eleven.' He seems to be concerned that time is short and I have been sitting on my ass doing nothing of any value.

'It is west of here and it has begun.' I can feel the formality capture my tongue and the diction and pace of speech is different. He looks at me a little differently. 'Let's go. We will need a car.' I am back in the here and now although I am unsure where we will be going exactly. Perhaps I will be able to feel him when we start moving.

'Jeremy, we are heading west. Find out the nearest old church in that direction.' I speak quickly into the phone, he needs to deliver or we will lose the vital moments that might be the difference between an innocent slain and a battle lost.

I start striding up the Cathedral flagstones and out into the night, I can't wait on DI White to find a car and I am drawn off up the High Street, or Royal Mile as it is called; he will just need to catch me up. The pull at me is very clear I am heading in the right direction. It feels like a chord being plucked on my spider's web of psychic energy. The pressure is building as the ritual is begun and I know that time is growing short. I cannot afford to miss this confrontation, Margaret needs me her name coming unbidden to my mind. Her terror is like a cold wet blanket clammy and chilling to me and yet arousing and gratifying to him.

The night is full of people, revellers out for a few beers and some carousing for the lucky ones. A few speculative glances in my direction at the crazy looking priest stomping up the street. The jeers of the drunkenly stupid reaching my ears causing my cheeks to flush hot with anger. I feel the need to retort but keep marching on. Where the hell is DI White? How long can it take to commandeer a police car? The answer isn't long in coming. He screeches to a halt beside me and I get in. He sets off, his heavy right foot causing a wheel spin on the slick cobbles that are exposed to the tyres. He doesn't fishtail the car but it causes a few of Edinburgh's denizens to get the fuck out of the way.

In seconds we are passing the Free Church of Scotland Church, St Columba's, and we are on the road down past the Castle mound. The high walls of the castle forbidding above us, perched like a black shadow scowling down at us. I am glad not to have had to attack that rampart. The feeling is changing as I feel the energy building to my right and now behind us. There are no old churches behind us on that side, just the castle.

'The church is on the other side of the Castle. Probably St John's on the corner of Lothian Road or maybe St Cuthbert's?' I know both of those having spent many an hour there. They have great coffee. White punches the siren and the lights begin to strobe. The road goes past the kings stables and the exorbitant car park that was built deep underground. Everyone obligingly pulling over as DI White mounts the kerb and makes a path that will take us to the lights and Lothian Road. He is driving like a madman and I hope we will get there in one piece; although with what awaits us at the other end I doubt we will be in one piece afterwards anyway.

Screaming tyres as we swing across the cross hatched yellow junction have me hanging on for dear life. The force of the turn throwing me against the door and it is then I regret the lack of the seat belt. Too late to put it on now, we will be stopped in a minute. The thrashing of the engine sounds impressive as do the screeching brakes telling everyone that this is a police emergency; as if the modulating siren and bright blue strobes didn't tell that story already.

'Less than a minute Father.' DI White has a solid grip on the wheel as we bounce and slide up on to the pavement along side the black metal railing that lead up to the massive spired church of St John. The slippery pavement caused the car to scrape along the railings leaving an interesting smear of paint on the iron and stone. The dents in the door and quarter panels pretty impressive, he hasn't missed any on his side. The headlight might be buggered as well; a full house. We get out like Starskey and Hutch sprinting towards the doors.

Chapter 27

I run up to the old wooden doors, re-varnished and pale in the street lights. I shove hard with my shoulder expecting them to open under our arrival. The solid thud and numbing of my shoulder reminders that I am not superman. DI White is on the radio calling for keys and someone to open the church. I notice he wasn't dumb enough to try the doors. Obviously it is a rookie mistake to make; well too bad I made it.

There is another door facing on to Princes street and I slip and slide around the corner before rattling the old heavy metal ring handle. Locked and no sign of anything happening inside. I can feel myself getting a bit frantic as I charge back to DI White as he stands outside the front doors. We are drawing a crowd of semi-interested onlookers, some of them with phones pointed in our direction.

I catch my breath bent over with hands on knees, adrenalin making me breathless. DI White 'Fifteen minutes for the keys.' He has had an answer and it doesn't present much chance of being in time.

'There is a door on the terrace that might be a better chance. Come on.' I drag him down the worn steps ignoring everyone and everything else that might be around us. I wonder if the car will be nicked by the time we get back. I stumble along my shoes slipping on the traction free flagstones causing me to slip and slide like I am Bambi on ice. I wonder if the terrace door is susceptible to a kicking in. One look at it tells me that I'd need a battering ram and a team of burly soldiers to have any chance. Churches sometimes had to hold the mob outside and generally the doors reflect that level of sturdiness.

'We will have to wait for the keys.' DI White is rattling the handles like he expects the door to just open under his touch. It doesn't, obviously.

'We will be too late then. I don't feel him here. Perhaps St Cuthbert's is the site.' I look from the terrace down into the darkness of Princess Street Gardens. The church is the dark shadowy shape overshadowed by trees. It has it's own graveyard and is pretty old. I have no idea if it is or isn't suitable, all I know is that this isn't the place. I can feel nothing at all from inside or even having been here. There is still about twenty minutes until midnight and the culmination.

'We need to go down the park steps to get to St Cuthbert's. Are you sure?' DI White is looking at me, worry beginning to pinch his features. We are so grasping at straws and he knows it.

'Give me a moment.' I try to gather myself, if I can't get some equilibrium it could be happening behind me and I would feel nothing. I take a deep breath and ignore the fire in my knee joints. I open my spirit to feel around me and aim my thoughts at St Cuthbert's with its pretty spire and cupolas visible above the darkness of the trees. I feel nothing from there either.

'Where the hell is he?' I can feel sod all and time is running away like sand through my fingers.

DI White is looking at me with horror, or is it revulsion. 'Are you all right? Your nose is bleeding.' Bleeding doesn't really cut it as I wipe a black bloody sludge from my nose. The smell is of rot and I throw up spectacularly over the terrace railing and the splatter patter of it landing on the stones below would have impressed me had I been watching. Snorting and coughing to get the gloop out of my nose causes a secondary round of retching and vomiting that coats the old iron railing that I am hanging on to. All the way down the lower half of my trousers is a viscous bloody smear that has them plastered to my hairy legs.

'Keep your nose out, Priest.' Reverberating in my head. A message from the enemy and he has given himself away. The attack pinpoints him where before I could not find him under some sort of spell. I grin at DI White.

'I know where he is.' I look up and high above us is the castle. Edinburgh Castle, world heritage site and unconquered it is in great condition; housing all sorts of artefacts and more importantly the Chapel of St Margaret. The Chapel sits inside the inner walls high above us, it is very old and perfect for Basomel. I snort out the last vestiges of the bloody snot like a professional footballer, one blast from each nostril.

'It is in the Castle.' I start running for the car, DI White doesn't ask any questions and gets to the car ahead of me, shouting at the spectators to get out of the way. Leaving the blue lights on attracts a crowd apparently.

'We need the castle opened.' DI White is shouting into his radio set, I am struggling to get the seat belt to stop locking and decide it will just get in the way anyway. I stop fighting with it and we are moving, lights and siren filling the night and causing everything to get the hell out of the way. The engine sounds so loud inside the car and I realise that the last set of kerbs we bumped over may have ripped off the exhaust. Looking out the rear window tells me a story. It isn't exactly ripped off just being dragged underneath and causing spark showers and a racket.

'Nearly there.' DI White is weaving all over the road as the car becomes a little less happy at his driving. The hard left turn at the mini-roundabout bounces his side against the tiered stone kerbs on that side of the street, they create a bumper that throws us back into the road. The cobbles all slick and slippery are for tourists and marching soldiers not half wrecked police cars.

'Thank God.' I want to be funny but I am clinging to the door handle and am braced into my seat ruing the lack of the seatbelt after all. The street leading up to the castle is old and narrow. The violence of the siren and blue lights driving everything ahead of us like a panicked herd of cattle. People squeezing into doorways and screaming in terror. Not just the women either, I joined in as we near-miss a crowd of revellers walking arm in arm down towards us.

In what seems like an eternity we burst out on to the esplanade where they have the Military Tattoo here every year. It is a huge space and White just guns the engine harder as we speed towards the drawbridge and the huge gates scattering the temporary barriers like skittles and dragging them along under the car. Naturally the gates are still shut.

The Chief Super better deliver or the mad driving will have been in vain. The screech and grinding noise as we pull to a stop is impressive as we throw open the doors and run for the gate. The headlights like two on-stage spotlights, creating fantastic shadows against the old oak and iron gates.

'We need this gate open now.' I shout at DI White because it is obviously his fault. He is already speaking into the radio. Professional call sign and requests for action and not a 'Get the fucking door open' anywhere in the conversation.

I am banging on a bit of door without black iron reinforcing studs, I would like my hands to work for the rest of my life, however short it might be. 'Fuck.' I roar in frustration, I look round and am temporarily white-spotted by our headlights.

'Garrison Sergeant on his way down with the keys, ETA less than a minute.' DI White is repeating the message I can hear perfectly well coming out of his radio. I can feel the growling in my throat as my impatience is getting to epic proportions. I stagger back as if a blow has just landed on my chest.

In St Margaret's Chapel the sacrifice is awake. I feel her terror and I know that Basomel is loving it. It fills my head, her screaming 'Noooo' and the view from her of the sharp fangs and red scaled skin. She is so young, probably eighteen but maybe not. I can see through her eyes the talon rip away the white spandex top barely caressing her skin. The little red lines not yet yielding blood. Basomel stills her with a stare, her bladder empties all over her legs and short skirt. I feel him swell with power and the burn of lust.

The rumbling of the heavy lock brings me to the gate once more. Slowly it opens enough to let us through and I sprint inside leaving DI White to tell the Gatekeeper something. He can tell them whatever he likes I am running up the steep flint-like cobbles and find that the years of avoiding exercise might just cost this young woman her life.

Puffing and panting and every ounce of oxygen feeling like a knife in the chest, I manage to make most of the first climb emerging from a tunnel onto the main path behind the battery terrace. I have been here many times and Mons Meg sits there like a monster cannon, the newer one-hundred-and-five-millimetre field gun delivers the percussive one o'clock salute every day. I wonder if I can use it to destroy the Demon. I can bet that has never been tried before.

My mind drifts as I try to avoid the agony of the ascent, knowing all the while that I may be too late. The sweat clinging all over my body is chilling in the wind and completes the discomfort my flesh is enduring. Past the museum and on to the inner ramp and under the inner Bailey gate. I am almost at the flat bit of the interior when my knees collapse and I run my face, chin first over the ground. The ground coming up to meet me so fast. The chain that keeps visitors from restricted areas invisible in the dark the cause of my fall, not exhaustion; although it must have been very close as to which would get me first. I groan and hold in the desire to squeal in agony.

DI White is helping me to my feet, probably because he doesn't know where the Chapel entrance is. Up the steps and along the high wall to the end. I can't actually force any words out at the moment, so he will have to follow me. I notice the knees are out in my trousers; another uniform destroyed in the line of duty. I doubt the bloody mucus and vomit would have come out anyway. I stumble using hands and almost on all fours to get up the flight of uneven, worn steps to the wall. The battlements look out over a twinkling city below, full of beautiful well-lit monuments and architectural wonders. Tonight I just need some air in my lungs.

DI White has no requirement for oxygen apparently and he is running towards the Chapel of Scotland's Saint, Margaret not Andrew. There is light from candles twinkling in the pebble glass panels that have filled what was once an open window. The screaming has commenced again and I try to make my knees bend and move but it is a struggle. White has kicked open a very heavy door, which is impressive but foolhardy. He throws his salt inside, in one go. I know this by the scream that erupts from the lips of our salt averse Demon. He charges inside, bravery seems to be built in with duty to protect and serve, and from what I guess was a demonic backhand, he flies back out through the doorway and off the walkway onto the grassy bank below. On the inside luckily, if he had gone over the battlements he would be a posthumous holder of whatever commendation policemen get.

    I advance as fast as my tortured limbs will allow, Basomel can feel me approach and I can feel his uncertainty. The air as thick as soup as I choke on the heady power cocktail of fear and blood that Basomel so enjoys.

Chapter 28

The door slams shut before me. The diagonal strips of very old timber and the regularly painted black gloss diamond shaped iron studs prevent my shoulder being used to force my way inside. I grab the handle and push, the door grinds open slowly, something metal is scraping over the grey flagstones. I see inside, everything etched permanently in one flash. This little chapel, at the top of the fortress, would have been an austere place to come to pray. The chill from the stones would pass all the way up your legs making them ache. Suffering for faith before a beautiful little stained glass window that would be backlit on sunny days. Although these are few and far between in Scotland.

The altar, although in reality not much more than a block of basalt on which the castle sits, is covered in candles. Thick candles that smoke and reek telling me they are tallow not wax; and the tallow used is probably human. On the altar a number of offerings, bloody and dried out organs ripped from the victims of his spree. The final offering lying stunned from a blow to the side of the head, is before the altar. Her pale flesh bruised and abused; legs bruised and grazed from being dragged along by the hair. Her young face swollen on one side where a slap has been given, a slap like no man could ever deliver. The power of the blow has probably cracked her cheekbone.

Between her legs, his back exposed and his haunches moving forward is the enemy I seek. Luckily she is out of it, the pain would be excruciating and he is not gentle. The echo of a previous recipient jars my insides recalling the wreckage he wrought inside her. The folded wings protecting him from me, like a leathery armour. The stench of his ardour and flesh filling my nostrils, not making me gag but spurring my hands to action. The casting of salt brings a scream that shatters the glass pictogram of the cross. I have air in my lungs and God is with me.

'I cast you out, foul spawn of the other-world. Go back to the pit made for you and your Master. In the name of Christ I abjure you.' The criss-crossing of the salt scarring and scalding the wings on his back causing them to spasm. The candles are buffeted and their light extinguished in the blink between words. In my hand the salted whip, I don't recall pulling it from my pocket. I pull my arm back and swing, in the dark anything could happen. Indiana Jones I am not and the first blow slides across the enemy causing pain but not much more. More like a pointless slap but causing pain due to the salt I soaked into the leather.

'In the Name of Christ I command you. The blood of the Martyrs condemns you and the power of God compels you. Return to the abyss and trouble this world no more.' My voice is like thunder in such a small place. I feel my words land like blows driving him back towards the altar. His hulking form flinching before me and recoiling from my whip. The whip that I am flailing about in spasmodic flicks. One flick lashes across his cheek landing like a deliberate blow, bringing a screaming roar of pain. I close in with salt running out but still scalding him. His rising scream suggests that some coated his sticky phallus and has got to smart. His frantic rubbing at the area would be comical in a different setting. A smile of grim satisfaction fills my face.

The girl lying on the floor chooses that moment to close her legs and roll away causing me to trip and stagger into the wall. Basomel flees past me towards the door. Escape his only thought as his inner cowardice in the face of the Lord comes to the surface. He reaches the door, staggering under the pain of the salt and the lash. His taloned hands ripping the door from the frame, so great is his desire to get away from me and the power of God. The discarded door clatters on the floor louder than a thunderclap in such a small place. The path to his freedom and the outside now clear.

I throw a vial of Holy water as hard as I can smashing it above his head on the stone lintel, its contents cascading and sprinkling the Demon. His cowering under the shards and burning, hissing liquid gives me a moment to get back to my feet. The girl has rolled away and is in a curled ball to the side of the Altar as far as she can be from the demon. I don't blame her. The ritual disrupted we need to destroy him before he escapes into the night.

'You are going nowhere ya bastard.' I hear DI White's voice from outside, as he tries to prevent the murderous fiend from escape. He is brandishing a handful of salt like a talisman. He needs to throw it straight in its face. His hesitation I hoped wouldn't prove fatal. I stumble forward, slipping on the scattered candles rolling about in the dark under my feet. Making my movements like a trainee stilt-walker on the wet cobbles; all legs and stumbles but I managed to keep upright enough to see DI White backhanded by a heavily taloned hand, launching him from the battlements once more.

Basomel jumps up on to the crenellated wall and in a moment of smug triumph, screams defiance in my direction. My whip hand flying forward, the salted leather wrapping around his neck as he threw himself from the wall. The biting salt causing Basomel to plummet on the far side of the wall. In that split second I know I should have let go. I didn't and the law of physics caused me to be dragged over the battlement like the tail of a roller-coaster, plunging over the inner wall onto the grass-covered rock below.

A thirty foot drop onto padded rocks is not something I would recommend but thankfully I had a large, taloned and fanged landing cushion. The whip entangling both of us; trapping me and burning him, has us rolling over cobbles and gouging at each other like a pair of pub brawlers. I am trying not to get my throat ripped out as his talons start to shred my coat.

His fist glancing a blow on my shoulder causing me to slide across the slick, damp, cobbles and making me finally release the whip. His wings are hanging like a pair of limp curtains, not having survived the fall intact and his movements tell of other injuries. I am glad that I am not alone, because my body is one big throbbing ache.

I groan as he gets to his feet and staggers away from me. The steps to the Gun Terrace leading him down and out of sight, I know I need to follow him. This ain't over yet. Turning on to all fours I manage with a wince or two to get to my feet. I can't let him escape. His time all but over as far as the ritual is concerned and he has failed in that as far as I can tell. If I can't get him now then he will litter the city with corpses until he is destroyed. Only the ritual sacrifice was time bound, or at least to Jeremy it was.

I slip down the slippery steps catching myself on the handrails and avoiding another fall in the dark. Ahead of me Basomel is looking over the parapet for a means of escape. A bell chimes the first of midnight's tolls, at the sound his head spins round to glare at me. I smile back grimacing through the pain.

'You are fucked.' I whisper, before pulling myself

upright 'The power of Christ compels you to his will. This water, blessed and pure, casts you from this earthly realm. A place that is yours no more. I abjure you, foul fallen spirit of Hell.' I am advancing with each word, Holy water in one hand and presented crucifix of Our Lord in the other. My pains falling away into the background of my consciousness. I can practically feel its fear.

'I close the door that opened to let you walk among the living, thou O cast out and damned spirit. I am the word that seals the gate, the word that pronounces the sentence on you and those that seek to escape the Pit. I am the light that the Lord sets before you. I cast you from the lands of the living.' I cross the Holy water over the chest of the Demon. The screaming in my mind and in my ears like lancing talons of fire. His talons bury themselves in my back as I sear him with the Crucifix on his chest.

The blast of power released throws him backwards driving his curved claws deeper into my back. I don't know which screams are the loudest as we are catapulted over another wall, higher this time. An embrace that will be the destruction of both of us.

Chapter 29

Falling together, like Gandalf and the Balrog. His talons hooked deep into my back like a cat that is desperately trying to avoid a bath, so agony inducing and deep I am in a Zen-like state. The pain washing over me like a purifying heat, leaving my mind wandering at speed as the rocks of the castle mass race past us. I find myself wondering about DI white and if he survived. I am wondering what spin and story the Home office will put on this and how much video will leak into the social media streams of conspiracy theorists. A laugh, probably hysteria escapes my lips.

The futile flapping of ruined wings accompanies the fall of two mortal enemies in the eternal struggle. Is this one going to be a win for either of us? A score draw, so prized on the football pools of years gone by. The spite and malice of my dancing partner are like blows all of their own, his snapping fangs not quite reaching me as we fall. The smell of charring flesh surrounds us, the smoke making my eyes water, as I press deep the blessed depiction of Our Lord on the cross. The heat making it impossible to release my hold, burning my hand too.

It isn't the fall that kills you. The shuddering impact with the jagged rocks below the castle walls would normally be fatal in almost all cases. In my case I land on the sturdy, muscled body of demon flesh and as we fly on to the next impact am thrown clear of his talons with an agony filled scream. The sailing through the air a blessed relief from my enemy's caress and hold. I am sure he isn't too upset to be free of me. The crucifix is no longer in my hand although I am sure that won't matter as I find a birch tree slowing my progress to the ground. I fall the last few feet onto a muddy path that must be a short cut round the castle foot that the local kids probably use.

I am alive, and surprised beyond belief. The tolling of a bell somewhere dragging me back from a moment of lying face down in the mud, and to the present. Groaning as I move is becoming a habit but I can barely lift my head to see where Basomel is. I hope he is as wrecked as I am, or there won't be much of a contest in round three. This was a classic rumble in the jungle but, sadly, I think I am George

Foreman looking up from the canvas.

Escaping, the fucker is still moving, that is what he is doing. He is scaling a wire fence that leads over the tracks to Princess Street Gardens. I say scaling, it more or less crumples under the weight of his body. A dragging leg, bloody and scaled, showing his injured state. One of his wings has been ripped from his back by the black rocks of the castle, and the streaming ichor flowing from shoulder to hip gleams under the fluorescent orange street lights. I push my body a little further, getting my blistered hands beneath me to get me on to all fours. Crawling after him seems like the right thing to do but unless I get upright I will never catch him. It would be easier to lie here and wait for help to arrive.

I never really do easy, too stubborn I suppose. Amazingly I get one foot in front of another and zombie walk along the path towards the fence. I see Basomel entangled in the briar that fills the space past the fence. He is frantically trying to get through them and down on to the railway tracks. I start to feel in my pockets for anything that I can use in this fight. The salt is finished, scattered all over the chapel and his dick. The Holy water is gone, two shattered in my pocket and others already splashed on his hide. Crucifix, gone, was embedded in his chest and might be there still. My Indiana Jones whip is between the upper walls I think.

I have smelly unction in a little jar but that's it. The prospect of getting up close and personal with Basomel again does not fill me with happy feelings. I trip as I near the fence. A green bottle, a Buckfast bottle to be accurate, a high caffeine-alcohol mix that is a staple of kids these days, causing my trip. In my day it was Diamond White cider but this is now the fortified wine of choice that is consumed all over the central belt. I scoop it up, my intentions to bottle the bastard.

Basomel is nearly free of the grasping thorns of the briar patch, and will be able to jump the last five feet down into the railway cutting and the tracks below.

I manage to get round the side of the tangle and am going to catch him one more time. I feel a rage burning in my chest, making me forget the agonies I will feel later. I charge, more a lumber but you get the idea, crashing the monk-made empty bottle on the Demon's head. It shatters spectacularly leaving me a jagged stabbing weapon that I force deep into his chest. It shatters into his flesh and mine. We have a synchronised screaming moment before I shoulder him as hard as I can, knocking him onto the tracks below.

I manage to avoid the last little fall, hanging over the wall edge topped with dress bricks, I am done. There is nothing left in my tank for this night. I bottled him like a street thug but he is still moving, the bastard just refuses to die. He stares up at me, we are both fucked. Is he considering ripping my head off, I hope not because right now all I could do would be to watch. We have a moment of understanding; the eternal battle rages on and we are just expendable meat sacks that are the proxies.

I pull in a hot gasping breath and realise I shouldn't have.'I abjure you, you fucking scumbag.' I manage a whisper but it might have been a shout as he flinches away from me. 'In the name of the Father, the ' I start to cough before I can finish. A rumbling noise fills my ears and a screech of hard metal filling the night as a very startled train driver tries to halt his Scotrail diesel-electric hybrid engine and the two carriages, that constitute the last train to Dundee, before impact with an unexpected object in the tracks.

The driver fails and Basomel decorates the front of the train and is dragged under the wheels that finally finish his time in Edinburgh. The screaming face of the driver is muted by the thick glass and the juddering halt of the train causes the lights to flicker on and off before going out all together. The emergency lights come on and I can see a number of faces pressed against the window trying to see what is going on. Bugger, one of them is pointing at me. I hope they can't see my dog collar or it will be more press for the Bishop to suppress. Although, to be honest, I don't really care any more. I need a rest and the brick wall feels so comfortable.

My phone is buzzing in my trouser pocket. It takes me a few moments to realise that is what the noise and vibration is. Groaning as I reach down, every inch a torture of fire on my back. I dig it out and look at the screen. The black blob obscuring the caller and cracks all over the screen tell me that it is as wrecked from the descent from the castle as I am. I press the button and press it to my ear. Speaking is a bit of a stretch at the moment so I wait.

'Father Andrew? Where are you?' Jeremy sounds

frantic. He really isn't cut out for this type of excitement.

'I am having a lie down at the train tracks below the castle. Basomel just stopped the train.' I manage a whisper and I hope heard me because I am not repeating myself.

'I will send help. Are you okay?' He manages to gush down the phone and pissing me off. I am really an ungrateful sod. He is going to have someone come and save my ass and I get pissy.

'Not really. Hurry up.' I lie back watching the stars above the castle. The are so clear and sharp, I hadn't really noticed them before. I am cold.

'Make a hole.' I hear a voice in the darkness. There are lots of noises but I can't seem to really get a grip on them. I can't make them into a coherent picture. 'He's lucky to be alive. People jump off that part of the wall to kill themselves.' Another voice but I can't summon the energy to be arsed to respond. A few jolts and a slamming of doors and it is quieter, thankfully.

'Can you hear me Father.' Firm but not shouting in my face. Obviously I can as I am not deaf. It seems that my body is basically inert and a cause for concern. My eyes are so heavy that I will open them later. I so want to be left in peace.

'Father can you hear me?' Again with the urging. I am sure he means well but, frankly, he is getting on my nerves. My eyes flicker, involuntarily as I try to sleep, causing him to prattle on about Lord knows what for what feels like an eternity.

We are nearly there, or so he says and has been saying for sometime now. It must be an Edinburgh thing; nearly there is very elastic in these parts. A cough escapes me and the pain lancing me hurts like the devil, causing me to groan inarticulately as the ambulance pulls to a halt. The cavalcade of medical staff and porters wheel me away to the innards of the hospital. Why do they keep peeling my eyelids up to shine bright white lights in? I am being assessed, apparently. Poked, prodded and stared at by worried faces, if they match the worried voices that I can hear. Hustle and bustle surrounds me but I am not really with it. I have no idea what they are doing to my body but I know I don't like it. The words are less distinct now as the team prepare me for something. I feel a bit spaced out, not in a bad way all things considered. The pins and needles sensation on the tip of my nose is a weird sensation and I smile.

'Father Steel, glad you are still with us.' A woman's voice speaks quietly near my ear 'You have had a fall and we are a little worried about the bump on your head. We are heading to theatre in a few moments. Just relax and we will take care of you.'

They say nurses are angels, well this one's voice had power and I believed her that everything would be all right.

'Special Branch. Anyone that doesn't need to be here; Out.' The barking of orders second nature to the owner of that voice. I can't imagine too many times when immediate compliance doesn't occur either. I manage to open one eye, a little like winking but really because it is too much effort to open both. Four burly, armed, Special Branch officers have moved to take over.

Hustling everyone out; except a nurse who is next to me and a white-coated young doctor with fuzz on his chin. He is objecting but they are ignoring his ineffectual demands to stop. Of all the times I have wanted to call in Special Branch and this is the one I get; I can't even enjoy it. I manage to keep watching from my restricted vision seat.

Enter stage left a middle-aged, little woman in green coveralls and head cover; a mask dangling below her chin and her clogs clattering on the floor angrily. 'Get your guns and stupidity out of my theatre.' She snarled like a pit bull causing everything to halt mid-step. I would have laughed but that was a stretch. In moments I am wheeled away missing the eyeball to eyeball that must have ensued. The soft angelic voice reached my ears just as they started the anaesthetic.

'You'll be fine. She's the best neurosurgeon in the country. Relax and I will be here when you are done.' I try to smile or at least I would have wanted to. I was out as her words finished feeding through to my brain.

Chapter 30

'You should see the other guy.' DI White makes light of the swollen, purple face mask he is wearing on one side. He does look frightful but I suppose I don't look great either. He eases himself into the visitor's chair, moving looks difficult for him too. The dynamic duo, that's us, got our asses handed to us on a silver platter. I manage to twitch my face into, what might be construed as, a smile. I am actually pleased that he is here and in one piece, more or less.

'I did, he wrestled a train and that didn't end too well.' I go for dry sarcasm because laughing hurts too much and the draining tubes move if I do. I have a lovely set of punctures in my back, a full set of ten, that have taken some explaining and have been problematic for the medical staff. The cracked ribs are a minor problem by comparison.

'I don't remember anything after I got this.' He points to the contusion on his face. He had a brief fall and a collision with the courtyard so I am not surprised that he recalls nothing.

'I decided to fly off the battlements attached to a demon by a length of leather. I am never using a whip again.' I grin, trying to make light of the life flashing by in an instant. The look on his face is comical.

'Then, because we had so much fun, Basomel and I decided to jump from the Gun Terrace in a suicide pact. Luckily I landed on him. Not many people survive that fall I hear.' Dead pan delivery minimising the terror that I felt and the fact that I was lottery-winning lucky to survive.

'Dear Lord, that is incredible. You are so fortunate that you aren't a smear on the path. How did the train get him?' He really wants to know. I don't blame him, I think he expects magic or something. He will be so disappointed by the last bit.

'I bottled him with a buckle bottle and shoved him in front of the train.' That pretty much covers the details. I look straight in his eyes daring him to disbelieve me. He erupts in a welcome laugh. He believes me and yet can't believe that a Priest Buckie'd a demon or that I might know how.

We look at each other, veterans together and both sure in the knowledge that this isn't over. The Demon has been vanquished but that doesn't end it. We need to find the summoner and cut the head off this particular snake. A snake that I have, frankly, no idea how to find. The snake might not even be in Edinburgh. I let myself lie back on my padded back, feeling a little twinge as the stitches are compressed.

'How do we find out who caused this?' DI White asks after a few moments of easy silence. It is good that he can cope with silence because often I lapse into it as I try to find out what is going on. That and the fact I have pretty piss poor social skills and often don't try very hard.

'Jeremy and his books are very useful, allegedly, for this sort of thing. He will be able to find some obscure snippets that will help us just enough to stumble on to a resolution.' I wince as I lever myself round a bit. The light-weight plaster cast on my left wrist supporting another of my falling injuries. 'One thing is for sure the enemy will get a head start on us. I am going nowhere for a week at least and you look like a few days would be a good idea.'

DI White nods his agreement before making his goodbyes. I doubt he will be off work for more than a day, after all what else does he do? It isn't like he makes model air-planes is it? His movements tell me just how hurt he is, falling twice on to flagstones, and that he will be a little slow for a while. He was lucky all the same.

Hospitals used to like to keep injured people in the wards for days at a time but that has all changed. The ward sister was in my room just a few hours after DI White telling me to get up and move around. Doesn't she know how injured I am? She took no nonsense either, dragging me out of the bed and taking me down to the common room where other patients gathered. All on the pretence that she needed to have my linen changed and I needed to be ambulatory. Apparently that's the same as walking about with my stand thing with the drain on it.

I am shuffling along like a geriatric and finding the lifting of my feet a trial. I feel the sweat beginning to bead on my brow as I struggle with the effort. The aches and pains trying to tell me to stop and go back to bed but my care-provider is having none of it. I groan like a sick goat a few times as I mince along the corridor.

'You need to keep moving or you will seize up and that'll take much longer to recover. Just take your time and we'll be fine.' She is trying to be helpful and professional so I don't tell her to piss off and leave me alone. We reach the common room with chairs tables and a television. More importantly there are newspapers and no other patients, yet.

I stand next to the table, abandoned by my nurse for the moment and look at he front page. 'Deer menace causes train disruption.' I almost laugh out loud but I know that will hurt so I hold it in. Deer? Which rocket scientist dreamed that one up. Like a deer is seven feet plus with wings. Anyway it seems to have had good coverage on all the papers.

'Princess Street Gardens to have deer cull.' I mutter a little under my breath, I didn't think there were any deer in the gardens or anywhere in the city centre. People will believe anything I suppose. Anything more reasonable than a demon was finally destroyed under the wheels of the late train to Dundee.

'Terrible isn't it.' A younger female voice wafts past my shoulder, obviously referring to the impending cull of Bambi and his family. I turn my head slowly to see a student nurse, I think, peeking past me a t the headlines.

'Absolutely.' I agree with her although I suspect

there will be no cull, ever. I am too tired to really play nice but I suppose that I should at least try to be civil. 'The deer caused an inconvenience so the council decides they need to be exterminated. Ridiculous, isn't it.' I manage almost a coherent viewpoint.

'Outrageous, they could at least just move them somewhere else. It can't be that difficult. Do you want tea or coffee or something?' I mumble back coffee and she leaves me to look over the rest of the paper. Not much of any real note inside the tabloids apart from a bit about 'The Graveyard Slasher' and continuing enquiries. The story will slowly wind down until we find a suitable patsy to pin it on. Preferably a dead one or a made up one. The facts are certainly not going to get in the way of tying that one up at a later date.

The hot steaming cup of freeze dried granules arrives as I am easing my ass into a comfortable looking high backed seat. I can get a good view out the window and also get a decent view of the television. I'll bet this is a popular seat among the inmates. Although I am not turning on daytime television. I don't think I could take a nuts and sluts production, ghoulishly watching other peoples dysfunctional lives played out in front of an audience. Who thought that would be a source of entertainment? Some heartless bastard in a suit, I expect.

'Do you need anything else?' She smiles at me again, leaning forward to make me comfortable when a pendant swings into view. I wasn't looking down her top, which on another day I might have. The silver and onyx twinkling caught my eye. I have seen one like that before. I know I have and I know it is important, I just don't know why.

'A lovely necklace, where did it come from?' I blurt out, hopefully she doesn't think I was perving her and sneaking a peek. She smiles and rolls it between her fingers.

'I bought it at a shop in the Grassmarket, it sells all sorts of unusual things.' She seems at once pleased I noticed and embarrassed that it was from an alternative shop. Does she know I am a priest? Is that the source of her discomfort?

'It looks lovely, does it mean anything?' I wonder if it is sold as a trinket or as a symbol of something or other. She is still running it along the silver chain and thinking about her answer, as if trying to recall what she was told at the time.

'I think it is some sort of good luck charm but I bought it because it looked nice.' She lets it drop back behind her top. She dismisses any importance of the pendant as she has settled me and is moving on to her next charge. I sit back and sip my coffee.

Having something to think about is probably a good thing for me. It will stop me just sleeping the time away in a fugue of boredom. The necklace intrigues me the Grassmarket has a number of 'Alternative' types of shops and our enemies might be hiding there. Shops where the more mainstream alternative lifestyle things come into the light of day. In the past it would have been bondage or adult products or seedy sex shops but nowadays New Age religious paraphernalia can be found. Everything from singing bowls for Buddhists to Wiccan and occult things. Mostly just harmless tat but sometimes items of significance can be bought. The rare and antique book shops are a particular source of interest and can be an afternoon stealer as I have found on more than one occasion.

I wonder where I might have seen one before, and after a good twenty minutes of racking my brain for anyone who might wear one that I might know, I resort to thinking about the women I have associated with recently. It is a short list and it pulls up nothing at all. I can feel my irritation rising when inspiration strikes. I shuffle back to my room, dragging my stand with the drains attached, I need to phone DI White. I am blissfully unaware of the arse-hanging-out nature of the hospital gown until I feel a cold draught caressing my downy cheeks.

'White? Steel here. Did any of the victims have a pendant? A silver and onyx pendant?' I forgot the small talk stuff again but if I am right then we have a lead. A possible line of enquiry as he might say. He is shuffling papers about and scanning the boards. I didn't think it was that hard a question.

'Jill is nodding at me. A squiggly shaped thing? Black and silver?' He is looking at the picture of it I bet.

'Sounds like it. I have a clue as to where it might come from. Can you check and see if any more of the victims have one? It may be the thing that links them all together. I think they may have been picked for slaughter.' I am stretching a bit but I'd bet I will be proven right. I need to sit on the bed all the nervous energy used up leaving me wobbly.

'Father Steel, you need to rest.' I have been rumbled by the nursing staff, no doubt I will be removed privileges of a phone.

'White aren't you meant to be at home?' I realise he is at work while I am incarcerated. It isn't fair.

Chapter 31

I am not good at recovery. Although these days I seem to be getting a great many more opportunities to practice the art of lying about and groaning like a sick pig. I get bored and then I get a bit cranky. Maybe that should be crankier. I have found that the quickest way to escape the nursing sorority is to be generally pleasant to them and then offensive as possible to the doctors. It seems that being crabbit to your nursing staff can result in unpleasant little experiences like hairs plucked by adhesive tabs. The bloke in the room next to me complains at the nurses all the time and has a less than pleasant time of it. His bed bath isn't nearly as warm as mine, I know because like all scamps we compare notes.

Badgering my doctor has been an effective ploy, he has had enough of my shenanigans and has sent me home to finish my convalescence so that my bed can be used for someone more needy. I am the picture of cheerfulness after his capitulation. Being back at the seminary does mean that I need to return each morning to have my wounds cleaned and checked. I am starting to move more freely now, like an eighty year old but still progress all ends up.

Bishop Michael was pleased that I survived my encounter and that the story of the deer on the track worked so well. He is less pleased that we had no idea what was going on. I have omitted to tell him of my current theory and my line of enquiry with DI White. We even have progress to report but I want to look for myself. PC Jill has been sent in on a couple of occasions to peruse the offerings and eliminate the stores that don't sell the right trinkets. We have narrowed our search and have been having the store, 'Bed knobs and Broomsticks' if you can believe it, watched.

Two weeks have passed since we had our tango on the terrace and DI White and I are going to have a look ourselves, his face is fully recovered and only a little yellow staining remains at the corner of his eye. I am much less recovered but my heavy coat hides my extra padding and my tentative movements suggest that I am a little bit fragile. I want to see for myself if this is the harmless front of trinkets it purports or if it is something more. DI White has been suggesting another week of convalescence before we do anything but I am too bored, or stubborn, to wait any longer.

The shop front is a natty red colour and the window is full of pagan symbology as well as the ubiquitous candles and gemstones. The black velvet covered window display furniture looks plush and the Athame (symbolic daggers) and crystals stand out clearly. The prices on little stickers are enough to make my eyes water, thirty quid for a small amethyst geode? I am obviously in the wrong line of business. The beaten copper singing bowl, small, has a price tag of nearly two hundred pounds. I feel my face twitching in disgust at the gullible nature of the customers of the shop. DI White whistles at the prices on the silver goblet on the right of the window display.

'Let's go. Don't break anything, we can't afford to pay for it.' I grumble as I reach out and push the door open. The tinkling bell sounding as we step inside. There is an open wood fire blasting heat into the main sales area, a black cat curled on the hearth sets off the tableau. It opens a lazy green eye and looks at me, I look back daring the little bastard to hiss. It doesn't, going back to sleep.

'Welcome to Bed knobs and Broomsticks, how can

I help you today?' The cheery young man is full of sincere teeth arranged into a disgustingly wholesome smile. He is tall, taller than me at any rate, and good looking which must help with the middle aged lady-desperadoes that no doubt are the core of the customer base. The younger goths will be interested too as will the rather omni-sexual dark masters, if any such frequent this place.

'We are just looking for inspiration for Christmas presents.' DI White lies smoothly as we start the wander through the sections of the small shop. The healing crystals and Moon charts all seem pretty tame but as we move into the bookcases we can tell the more serious aficionados would spend their time here. The books have very interesting titles and the price tags seem to grow exponentially as we go further.

I run my fingers along the spines of the books, just casually feeling my way around but there is nothing brewing so far. Paraphernalia of a variety of fashionable alternative religions and sects cover the shelves, themselves decorated by silver pen squiggles that mean absolutely nothing at all, and we come to the more recognisable occult items. Pentacles and chalices made of a range of metals adorn a bookcase;

shabby chic I think they call the worsted veneer.

A glass cabinet is mounted on the wall with a selection of, what must be, more expensive pendants and chains. I scan the offerings recognising the one that looks familiar; silver and onyx and drawing the eye. I wonder if it is enchanted to draw a certain client group. It doesn't work on me but it might give me an idea if I could touch it. Three of the victims it turns out had similar, unique, pieces that may have come from a shop like this. One definitely came from here, paid by credit card, but the others may have come from here but proof is difficult. We didn't search each woman's home for a necklace, nor did we explore the fact that our demonic friend may have taken the pendant on the ones that didn't have one.

'Can I look at one of these pendants please?' I motion to the young man who is trying hard to ignore us and read his phone. I am loud enough to get him over and soon he is opening the cabinet with a small key that is pretty fiddly or he is nervous. I reckon it is the second of these reasons.

'These look very interesting, you must sell lots of them.' I try to sound enthusiastic and unknowing as my fingers tease and examine many other pendants before nearing the one I want to test. 'I think Jill might like this one.' I say casually as my fingers lift the onyx and silver item from the velvet backing. I feel a tingle like a static pulse, trying to make me not want it. Presenting a negative impulse that would be a minor enchantment. This pendant is for young women alone I think. I let it drop back. 'Maybe not, it feels heavier than I thought. Thanks for showing me.' I make it clear that I don't want to buy it. Was that relief flashing across his young face? Or maybe I just want him to be guilty and involved.

'Do you have a website?' DI White distracts him as he fiddles with the cabinet and soon our server is off to get a card with the details. Once we have a moment alone, I nod telling White we are on the money. This is our place.

'Do you buy in your jewellery or is it made by yourselves?' I ask as I look at some pewter chalices and Wiccan items. I look up trying to see if there is any dissembling by the mouthful of teeth.

'We buy it in from local craftsmen and women. The details are on the website if you are looking for specific items. The bowls and such are bought in from farther away. The owners would be better placed to help with any specific enquiries, I just mind the store.' Another attempt to disarm and divert us. He wants us out for some reason. It is not as if we are in uniform, although maybe priests and coppers give off a vibe all the time anyway.

'Okay thanks. I will have a look online and see how we get on. We are local so I can always pop in another time.' I am getting into the role maybe I should be on the stage. We are back out the door and into the street wandering away casually across the road towards a rather busy looking cafe. I casually glance at the windows above the shop seeing a tell-tale twitch, we have been watched and probably rumbled. We head inside to formulate a plan based on what we know. Which isn't much.

Chapter 32

'The pendants are the key.' I start with the main thing, again no small talk as DI White puts our frothy Cappuccino mugs in front of us. I suppose I should have let him sit down first. Oh well, too late for a do-over.

'I thought they might be. I thought the one you wanted to check looked an ugly piece and I can't see why anyone would actually buy one.' He sips his mug, getting the inevitable froth on the end of his nose. You can't bring culture to a laddie from Oxgangs, you shouldn't even try.

'They are enchanted to be attractive to young women, I'd bet. When I touched it, it made me not want to buy it, a general negative reaction to it. It seems that these pendants were used to select targets. Maybe the beast was sent after the women wearing them. Why? I don't know but I am pretty certain.' I wonder if I should tell him about the nose froth. I sip mine, avoiding the adornment and I wipe my nose anyway, DI White surreptitiously wipes his realising he had been dipping his beak.

'It makes the shop a front and the toothy bastard an accessory to the murders. I think he would fold like a cheap card table if you lifted him.' Not that I am telling DI White how to do his job, well I am but I am being subtle about it. I slurp at the chocolate covered froth on the top of my coffee, culture Fife style.

'I doubt I could get a warrant for a search but we could ask him to come to the station to help us identify a number of items of jewellery. We could see if he denies they are from the shop.' DI White is being way to police-like for my liking. I want to just kick in the door and drag him away, Spanish Inquisition style. He is a minion and would probably lead us to the next step in the chain.

'We were watched as we left the shop, from the upstairs window. Do you think they didn't believe we were customers?' Hard to believe but I wonder if my acting career is in tatters after one bad review.

'I think they could tell we weren't just looking. People can usually spot cops a mile away. Probably picked you out too, your disapproval at some of the items might have been spotted.' He is gently suggesting that my face tells the world what I am thinking. What a shocking revelation that is.

'We will need to move quickly then, or they will be gone before we know it.' I swig my cup and avoid a runaway drip, seeing it hit the table and not my trousers. The aches in my back seem to be less now that I have an enemy to hunt.

DI White, pulls his phone out and starts dialling the station. No sooner the word than the deed, and he is planning to have this shop watched. DI Anderson being shanghaied into action to use his team. Possible drug ring running out of the shop is the excuse. It always gets the police to act if there is a chance of busting the supply chain. I decide to call in a favour as I get mine out, as it were. We are the picture of modern conversation both on our phones to someone else; first world problems eh?

'Jeremy, Steel here, How are you?' I start off a conversation, I surprise myself at times. Father Jeremy is a little bit down on himself after the Cathedral farce and the strip that Bishop Michael tore off him for his error, I have long since gotten over that mess. After all I had an interesting flight and my life flashing by was a great in flight movie.

'Fine Father Andrew. How are your wounds?' He

sounds a little bit nervous, like I am going to bawl him out for being wrong. If that was the case I would be on the receiving end ad infinitum. Never kick the puppies, they grow into great big wolfhounds with slobbering jaws full of teeth.

'Good Jeremy. I am well. I need a favour. Can you tell me if a pendant could be keyed for a demon to hunt? I have a picture that I can get sent to you? I have just been in a little shop of alternative religious artefacts and have discovered the enemy, I think. I knew what I was looking for and it felt like it was telling me not to buy it.' I know I am a bit garbled. It might just be easier for him to meet us.

'I am not really sure I know what you are asking.' He is hesitant, the Bishop must have really chewed him out. I have had that one and it ain't pretty.

'Can you come down and meet us? It might be easier, I need your expertise.' See, I can be nice. He needs someone to be on his side it seems. DI White is looking at me like I have grown horns. I frown at him as I end my call with Jeremy.

'What?' I look at him, not appreciating the little grin under his coffee cup. It is like I need to be a bastard all the time. He is laughing at my softer side;

I'll never hear the end of it.

'Better not tell the Chief Super that Father Jeremy is on the case. He demanded that 'the useless twat' be kept as far away as possible.' DI White is openly grinning now. I know my face is a picture that would curdle milk.

'Tough. I need his input and the Chief Super can suck it up.' I am openly grumpy now, probably because I know I will have to buy the next round of frothy artisan coffee at capitol prices.

In less than an hour we three middle aged technophobes are huddled around a pretty dodgy laptop looking at the website of 'Bed knobs and Broomsticks' on the free Wi-Fi from the cafe in which we are ensconced. Jeremy brought the tech and as such is the one touching the buttons. I can tell DI White is itching to get in and go much faster but he is managing to resist at the moment. I am bored watching their efforts and am keeping an eye across the road. The shop is still open with a very limited footfall. It can't be profitable, surely. It is as if people are encouraged to walk past, perhaps a minor enchantment to keep people away this afternoon.

'The pendants come from an artist in Mid Calder, apparently.' Jeremy has another tab open and another website slowly loading. The pictures would suggest that the artist is definitely on the alternative spectrum if the site décor is anything to go by. It seems to be all black and red and symbols of Goth persuasion, the artist is a young woman with those big ear spacers making big loops of skin from her earlobes; looks stupid if you ask me. She is adorned with pentacles and the usual stuff that those trying to be different all wear.

'It proves nothing really. She may have made them but whether she puts the enchantment on them is another thing.' I mutter quietly enough for my other two amigos to hear but not any further. DI White nods in agreement.

'It does give us a reason to visit, though. We could go out this afternoon and shake the tree?' He seems keen to get something happening and to get someone into the interview room. Something we agree on.

'This looks a bit interesting.' Father Jeremy is peering into the corner of the screen. I am at the wrong angle and can't actually see a damn thing. DI White is doing the peering thing too. It seems when they do that their brains and mouths stop working. I keep my irritation in check but it won't stay there forever.

'You are right, I thought it was just a mark on the screen.' DI White is pointing as he leans forward 'right click it.' They are disappearing down a techie rabbit hole and opening a new tab or something. I still can't see and decide that I might have a long wait if I don't move round; not that I expect to understand what I am seeing anyway. I decide that I might as well get another set of coffees for all the help I will be about a mark on the screen.

Twelve pounds eighty for three fucking coffees. Granted they are specially hand crafted, lovingly tended and blended by a barrister of impeccable skills and deft touch. It is still twelve quid for three coffees, I feel that I have been fleeced and I am smiling like a village idiot as I pay for them. Jeremy, I notice, has deep pockets and short arms as it never seems to be his round.

He and DI White are doing the heads together geekfest thing, a little club I will never be a part of. I try not to bang the coffees down like my mother used to bang our dinner plates down on the table, especially after she had been arguing with her boyfriend of the day. Passive aggressive sort of thing, or at least that's what the psychobabblists would call it.

It seems there is a little bit in the very corner of the screen that those in the know would know to click taking them to a special site, a portal Jeremy called it. He went on at length about some technical stuff that White seemed to follow with ease, I was lost at the Darkweb statement. I think they knew my nodding along was for show and that I had no idea.

'It is like a secret internet Father Andrew.' Jeremy is being patient with the child in the team. I nod but how can there be a secret internet? Wouldn't everyone just log in to it or something? What would stop them? Is there a special handshake? Like the online Masons? I think he has me rumbled as he carries on 'The more unsavoury characters hide on the Darkweb. The drug dealers, the pimps, the Satanists, arms dealers and the like.'

I think he may be exaggerating for effect but if I were any of those guys I would want to be on the secret web thing. It seems that the tracking is harder on the Darkweb than on the internet we all use. Surely the police are all over the naughty one? Going by the look on DI White's face it would appear not. He looks like a kid in the proverbial candy store.

'What are we waiting for?' I ask as they salivate over their discovery. Shouldn't we just get right in there?

'We need a login.' Oh that makes it clear then. Whatever a login might look like, we do not have one. Sitting here across the road from the bad guys nest of vipers and we are looking for a login or logon or something.

'Should I just go over and get one? Just kick in the door and terrorise the toothy twat in the shop?' I know that won't work but staring at a screen that says username and waiting will achieve eff all. Fuck my frothy coffee is cold. I drink it anyway, after all I paid for it.

Chapter 33

The head scratching continued until we were evicted from the coffee shop and had to decamp to the incident room. The room was still looking fully functional but the caravan of resources has moved on to another more pressing case and, while the cases remained open, the knowledge that the demon had been destroyed by the late train meant that the brass had redeployed everyone except DI White, spotty MacBride and PC Jill. We were huddled round a laptop with a tech support from central services that had been pulled in as a favour. He was a friend of Jill's and was only too happy to help her and, by association, us.

He had brought some electrical stuff and his pilot's case of tools but I think that was just for show as most of the time he was clicking his mouse and tapping the keyboard. He looked very young for this sort of sensitive work. I thought. Still, we would have been looking at the login screen all night with no progress if we hadn't called in some help. The Darkweb, would have remained dark and we would have been arrhythmic due to the consumption of coffee.

DI White and I plan a little visit tomorrow to Mid Calder to beat the bushes and see what slithers out from under them but we need a clue as to what to expect.

I think my two wannabe geeks are getting in the way of our imported one and I can feel my boredom threshold being threatened once more. I have busied myself with making coffee and reading meaningless reports but the make work has died off and now, watching three animated heads clustered around a laptop has lost the limited appeal it had in the first place. I resort to google to look at the artist's website and am randomly clicking on pictures for expanded views when I get a chat box open on my screen. I yelp like the kid who has just been pinged in class with a rubber band, all very manly.

'How can I help you today?' It reads and is simply the artists way of interacting with a client, probably on the website so long that it sets off alerts.

'Guys I might have something.' I try to sound casual but their interest was piqued at the yelp, I expect. Young David, as I think of him, moves quickly to put his finger over the webcam and turns off the speakers on the desktop. He puts his finger to his lip as he slips a piece of Duck-tape over the camera lens freeing up his finger. He is taking this seriously but I know he wants to tell me why this was important 'Webcams and speakers can be operated remotely over the web and any Darkweb criminal might have that capability.' It is like an episode of Spooks.

'What do we type back?' DI White asks and the blank stares all round suggest that coffee hasn't stimulated too many brain cells in our little group. I begin to type. It is a conversation after all.

'I am looking for a piece of jewellery, something unique and different. Special.' I speak as I type it, you know in that slow I am typing it type of voice. I have the keyboard so I am doing it. It isn't fast typing either and I can feel a number of itching hands wanting to take over. The amateur finds a lead where the techie brigade got nowhere.

'Is the piece for a man or a woman?' The little text box pings back at me quite quickly. I type quicker this time, 'Woman' but the keyboard is a bit crap so my woman has two 'M' in the middle and I resend without the typo. I know I will have to give in to the inevitable and let someone else type.

'Let Jill answer and see if they are trying to lure her in. This may be part of their targeting scheme. We might be able to set them up.' DI White speaks quite loudly, being only a few inches from my ear but he is right. Jill might just sound like the perfect target.

The little box has a lol in it as Jill gets settled in and David the techie disappears to his laptop to do something that I don't understand. Jeremy follows to watch the other screen as DI White and myself wait to give our, obviously, expert opinion on what the answers should be.

'Did you have anything in mind? Earrings? Pendant? Bracelet?' The artist can smell money or is it something else. Jill starts to type a reply, and her fingers are flying over the keys.

'I am looking for something for my girlfriend and myself that will be special to us. Pendants and bracelets maybe? Matching but not the same. I like silver.' Jill is good at this, or maybe it is just what normal people actually do. I would have been hard pressed to answer that with much more than a few words. This feels like a real conversation.

'So his and hers complementary pieces?' The

artist is trying to elicit the details so that she can make a recommendation. Trying to narrow down where to point her in a bid to present something appropriately expensive.

'Hers and Hers complementary pieces.' Jill drops her own relationship right in to the mix without batting an eye. From the stifled sounds and looks at the other screen neither of them were aware either. Maybe they think she is just playing a role.

'Okay that makes it easier to manage. I don't do a great many pieces for men sticking mainly to women's jewellery. Silver you said? For both?' The calm acceptance of the different relationship mix seems genuine, after all it is the modern world and marriage will soon be more than just between a woman and a man. Love is love, as all the churches should be proclaiming but aren't.

'Will I play along and see where she leads me?' Jill speaks directly to me then looks round at DI White, who is her actual boss. He looks to me to answer.

'Play along and see if she offers the kind of pendants that I think are key, and see where she wants to go. Who knows she might invite you out for a fitting or viewing or something. You are doing well.'

We should let her get on with it in peace, David says he will be watching on his cloned screen, whatever that is.

DI White and I move into his office to plan the next steps and options. That and have another cup of coffee which he starts the process off by filling the kettle from the bottled water dispenser. There are no actual taps closer than the toilets but the chilled plastic bowser is right outside his door. I don't think it is meant for coffee but needs must as they say.

'Can we have MacBride pull the shop assistant in to identify some pieces of jewellery tomorrow as we go on our field trip to Mid Calder? If we keep them both busy then they may be less able to react to what we are up to.' My planning skills coming to the fore in a blinding glimpse of the incompetent.

'We can, but I doubt we will discomfort them too much. After all there will be other staff to cover the shop and if there isn't we can't force him to come to the station.' The cold water rains on my parade delivered from a smiling assassin with a coffee cup. Luckily he has found some biscuits to soften the blow. I feel the frown settling on my face but we are making progress.

'Lets see what the artist throws up. If she is enchanting the pendants she is an accessory and a witch. If not she is just selling pendants to the shop and we can eliminate that line of enquiry.' I am learning this police lingo and sound like I belong here. Soon I will be proceeding along the road instead of going but that might be a while yet. Baby steps.

'I think you are right. This Darkweb portal bothers me more than a little as this could lead us into the lands of Serious and Organised Crime. They get a bit protective of anyone poking their nose into their turf. They won't want us buggering up their operations for a few pendants at an occult store.' He slops his coffee on his side of the desk and manages to restrain the expletive that almost got out.

'I hope David can get us inside and we can get a peek into their secrets. It might give us an edge on all sorts of things.' I think I get the idea of this web thing, but I might be a bit fuzzy on its usefulness. I doubt they have membership lists and a schedule of satanic events lying around.

'I hope he doesn't bollox it up. We will be in enough shit if we are caught tramping about where we aren't wanted.' He manages not to slop his coffee this time. The desk phone rings. We both look at it like it has grown spikes. It is after seven and no one would be expected to be here. I catch his eye, 'Brass?' I whisper as if they can hear me.

'DI White, incident room.' He turns on the professional I am in charge' voice and I almost feel myself sitting straighter in my seat. He seems to be sitting straighter too.

Chapter 34

I am pretty crap at hearing one side of a conversation. It is a failing of mine and the unhelpful contributions from DI White are about as illuminating as a torch with flat batteries. He isn't happy at the conversation but he is stoutly resisting the giving up of information. I don't think it is DI White's brass, just a generic brass trying to tell him what to do and like a good cop he is defending his turf. I huff a bit louder than I need to and DI White sends me the warning look, no one needs to know that I am there. Although I can pull my 'Do you know who I am card' if the caller starts to get shirty. I wait, badly, as DI White accedes to a demand to meet.

'Serious and Organised want to visit us. They are on their way over.' DI White doesn't look happy either, a pair of grumpy bookends we are. Will we have to put on happy smiles when they arrive? Fuck that I have aches that give me a pass. That and a cast on my wrist that marks me as walking wounded.

'What do they have to do with this?' I can't really

see that this has anything to do with them. I am trying to catch a satanic demon summoner; serious I can agree but organised crime I sincerely doubt.

'Nothing but they know we have been poking at the Darkweb portal on our system and got an alert. We will tell them as little as we can and get them to piss off.'

'Seems like a plan. Do we need to hide Father Jeremy? Perhaps in the cupboard at the back?' I keep a straight face and wonder if he knows I am almost joking.

Our friends arrive in less than ten minutes which makes me wonder if they used their sirens to get here. They are an odd pairing, one like a great big shithouse of a man and the other is a slight framed spectacle-wearing bloke with a fine fuzz on top of his head. The odd couple they are probably described as by everyone who meets them. They seem to have had the humour bypass that afflicts many who work in specialist departments containing the word 'serious'. I give them a bland look as they make themselves at home, proprietary bastards and not even a 'pleased to meet you' or a 'hello' to fill the air as we get ready for a less than cordial meeting.

'Special Agents Johnson and Johnson?' I ask, they won't get it but it gives me a little warm glow. I might need to give them some clues as to my humour. My face is in the blandest setting I can find that isn't hostile.

'DI White, thanks for meeting us at such short notice.' The little one is doing the talking, which isn't a surprise. He still hasn't introduced themselves to me; I am chopped liver apparently.

'Father Steel, these are DI Wilson and DS Baxter. They are from Serious and Organised Crime.' DI White does the introductions smoothly, giving nothing away to our new chums. I nod like I know which is which, although I don't really care. They look in my direction and barely a nod between them.

'DI White, why are your guys poking about on the Darkweb? We have a load of sensitive investigations that could be compromised if someone lumbers around too much.' I am sure that he is trying to win friends and influence people; straight out of Dale Carnegie.

'It is an active lead for us in a multiple homicide investigation.' DI White is totally cool and professional, he hasn't offered them coffee though. I decide that keeping quiet might be the best option for now but I doubt that will last long.

'Of course. We need to just make sure you won't get in our way. After all, we are all on the same side.' He smiles, well it was an attempt to be friendly but came across as condescending in the extreme.

'I am sure that your way is not anywhere close to our way so we should be fine.' Another bland statement from my boy, giving away nothing and still keeping the peace. I can feel a get stuffed building but I am holding it in. I focus on the details as they play the 'show me yours and I'll show you mine' game of cat and mouse. Wilson, the little one, is wearing cufflinks and not cheap ones either. His police-work doesn't involve poking about in grotty flats or dumpsters. His suit is a few cuts higher up any pay grade than I could afford and looks well tended and his shoes hand stitched leather. He is very well presented. We are the Crumpled Brothers by comparison.

The back and forth has brought us no closer to any meaningful discussion and I can feel my face hardening into the familiar frown lines, it won't be long before something escapes.

'White, we both know I can call your boss and get you yanked off this area. Tell me why you are poking about.' DI Wilson plays the 'my dad is bigger than your dad' card, which is my last straw.

'I can call mine and you wouldn't like that DI Wilson.' I let it float out across the room. The spinning exorcist heads of our two visitors is almost comical. They can't work out which boss I mean and need a double take.

'I'm sorry Father?' He tries to get a replay in his head and can't decide what I meant.

'I forgive you, DI Wilson. I said you don't want me to call my boss. Why don't you tell us where your active investigations cross over with a possible Satanist?' I manage to keep my voice even. Their faces look so comical though.

'Father I am sure you mean well but this is a police matter.' He tries some more condescension, which is probably the worst option he could have gone for. His day is about to go in a whole new direction.

'Why do you think I am here Inspector? I don't mean well. I am here to catch a killer and our killer is a Satanist.' I feel my irritation getting the better of me.

DI White gives me a warning look, it might be play nice or something like that. Too late for that, they are wasting our time and need to fuck off.

His face is a little flushed now, the unimpressive dog-collared spectator has teeth and attitude and he didn't expect that. He straightens in his seat, all pretence of cooperation and civility evaporating like the reek off a turd. His eyes narrowing as he turns his full attention on me. He doesn't know where I fit into this pantomime and he is a little unsure how hard to push his authority. One thing is certain he is not used to being challenged in his domain. A beat or two passes as he tries not to sneer at me. I wait, a little like a staring contest between five year old kids in a playground, until he has to speak.

'I appreciate your candour Father, but the police force has wider concerns to consider.' He begins. Apparently I am an idiot so I decide to let him continue; after all it is his career. 'DI White is not the senior officer here and I can have this investigation back away from any Darkweb entanglements and he knows it. Now Father, if you don't mind, we will resolve whether I let this little circus continue.' His arrogance is colossal and needs a little adjustment.

'DI Wilson, I will decide where our investigation goes. Unless, of course, you can convince my boss that you should be in charge. The Home Secretary always takes my calls. Should I call him?' The look on their faces is priceless; you can't buy this with MasterCard.

'I'm sorry?' DI Wilson has a wonderful level of incredulity in his voice. He is looking from me to DI White and is about to mount his response when my hand comes up cutting him off. I hand him a card. It will make his night I am sure. His gorilla is glaring in my direction which is meant to be intimidating.

'DI Wilson, I am here at the command of the Home office and have overall say in where our investigation goes. Crimes against the Church are my jurisdiction. If you feel the need have that checked out, go ahead but you know it would be a waste of time.' I pause letting my words find their way through the fog of his indignation. His face is turning that lovely blushing pink on the way to puce I expect. He is staring at the white card I have just handed him. After a moment he hands it to the gorilla, he doesn't say much either.

'So about this Darkweb thing.' I have given them as long as they are getting to catch up. 'In what way might you be encroaching on our investigation?' What a turn around for him to grasp. DI White is a great straight face player, he just waits letting the silence fill the space.

DI Wilson is trying to pull some coherence from his foggy brain, and is not really getting it together. He keeps looking at me and the card in sequence without making progress. He wants to check out my credentials but doesn't dare. He has no idea if I am a bluffer or not and that confusion is written large all over his face.

'DI White will keep you up to speed, Gentlemen. After all we are playing for the same team, are we not?' Wilson knows a dismissal when he gets one and the odd couple head on out, unhappy and unloved. I smirk at DI White who can no longer keep the grin from his police face.

'One nil to us, I think.'

Chapter 35

Mid Calder, as you might find out from Wikipedia, is not exactly a metropolis. It is one of three Calder villages which I almost never drive through on my way to Livingston and the mega shopping experience that is the Almondvale Shopping Centre. I always drive along the motorway and avoid all the little villages clustering near Edinburgh that once had coal mines and factories nearby. The stop-start nature of traffic light main streets make a simple journey tedious and almost interminable and that is why DI White is driving as I complain, not quite, incessantly at the time taken to get there. I am a little too old for 'Are we there yet?' but I can feel it coming. DI White doesn't seem to notice how long our drive into the central belt is taking. We have a sat-nav to take us in the longest possible route and the unmarked car is not in the greatest of condition inside. Hygienically speaking.

The winding route takes us out of the village to a farm track, with a road designed for bigger wheels than ours if the ruts are anything to go by. The intermittent scraping under the car suggests we might end up leaving the exhaust behind. The bouncing around is fun too until finally we each a better bit of gravelled road leading to a cottage with a few outbuildings. There are plenty of trees and hedges around making this very secluded. Perfect to prevent the nosiest of neighbours.

'We're here.' DI White with a blinding glimpse of the obvious. He parks the car on what looks like a solid flat bit but there is a great big puddle on my side. Bloody typical; I hope I don't have to wade too far. Luckily it isn't deep and I don't end up with wet socks.

The cottage looks well kept and has an arch at the gate, almost like a grannies cottage in little red riding hood. Roses without flowers are waiting for the next summer and the foliage has died back a bit. A sign on the gate tells us we are at the right place. The red painted door is all glossy and shiny, somebody cares to clean it. I wonder if the designer lives alone or with a someone. The little fence around the front garden is wooden but not painted white, a cliche avoided thankfully. I let DI White open the gate and I wander up behind him. The passing of the threshold tells me that this is definitely our place.

'White, this is the place.' I speak quietly letting him know that something might go down very quickly. After our last tag team efforts against a demon we need to be careful. It is daytime so I am less worried although I have an itch under the cast that is irritating me mercilessly.

He nods and knocks the door knocker. It is a brass fox head and paws that gives a loud rat-a-tat-tat as DI White knocks. We wait for what seems an age before DI White starts the peering in the windows thing that people do.

'Maybe in the workshop at the back?' I try to be helpful, sometimes. Anyway we can see nothing through the net curtains that obscure everything inside. At least we haven't started chapping on the glass going 'yoo hoo'. I wander back along the path noticing the mixtures of herbs and plants in the cottage garden. Companion planting it is called, where one plant protects the others by attracting the bugs and pests. Only in this case I think the planting is a bit specialised and may be more of an active herb and spell garden.

Moving like a pair of nonchalant delivery drivers looking for a signature we make our way around the back to the three outbuildings. They are decent sized former cow sheds and farm buildings and all look used, if the doors and windows are anything to go by. I lead us over to the first one, no particular reason to do so, and try the handle. I am done with knocking and pretending we aren't here on my business. I have my hand in my coat pocket; a reassuring vial of holy water meets my fingertips. Locked and no sound from within, DI White is ahead of me to the next one.

Before I can warn him to be careful he has turned the handle and opened the door. I can't see inside but am moving quickly forward when I see him stagger out into the yard. In his gut a dark handled knife is lodged and the growing stain moving through his fingers and coating his trousers is not a good sign. He falls to his knees a few yards away and is groaning into his radio.

'Bastard.' I shout as I make my way into the doorway. The dim interior is a workshop to make jewellery and has a wide range of tools covering the benches. Perhaps I should have shouted 'Police' but it is too late now. The view I have of the long hair flying behind the enemy as she (it might be a he) passes further inside through a small door is fleeting at best. I snatch up a hammer like implement on my way past the bench. I have watched a load of action films and kick in the door that just slammed. When I say kick in, it flies in and off the hinges, maybe I have been a bit enthusiastic. The crashing and splintering of the wood sounds like a sound effect on a movie but inside is a little chapel of horrors.

A pentagram of silver on a black background, probably made of velvet, hangs against the far wall. The silver gargoyle-like faces holding it in their fanged mouths look sinister and vintage. The altar table is laden with the Satanists one-oh one-set, available from mail order in three easy payments of fifty pounds including post and packaging, and probably the booster sets too. The stone floor is swept to within an inch of its life, no doubt a regular chalking surface.

A young woman, maybe thirty, with long hair and a snarling disposition is chanting something at me. I am presuming it is a spell of some kind. She wasn't expecting the door to be in bits, I am sure and expected even less the hammer flying straight for her head. It seems to take her a few words to realise that the heavy lump of metal is aimed at her head. She stops mid stream to duck away from the missile that, incredibly, would have connected.

The tall floor-standing iron candelabra with fat black candles atop them gets the kick over treatment as I charge forward. I am going for a direct physical assault on this bitch. I have no idea whether she is a witch, priestess or dabbler but either way I am going to take her out.

A thick purple smoke starts to emanate from the floor as I scatter all the crap from the altar top. She is shouting words again, sounds like Latin to me but she is close by. The air is acrid and brings a watering to my eyes that is unhelpful if I am going to get her. Laughing, sinister and bitter, reaches my ears and a solid thud in my back throws me off balance, the smoke is coalescing into something solid. That something solid has just hit me.

The smoke filling the room like a gas canister escaping into space is making breathing impossible. I hold my breath and scramble away and try and remember where the door was. Another thud, this time on my shoulder helps me stagger through the space I made by removing the door. At least now I can get a breath, even if I can't see shit. I manage to get to the outside air and suck a huge lungful hoping to clear my head and stop the aching in my chest. I turn around, light behind me in the doorway, and realise the smoke stops at the door of the inner sanctum. A stand off of a kind, I cannot get in but it doesn't seem to get out either.

I look over at DI White, he seems to be holding himself together, the knife still buried in his gut. The red stain seems about the same size which I hope is a good thing. I retreat to where he is resting against the back wall of the house, my eyes focussed on the workshop as I make my way over.

'You all right?' I ask, not looking down at him just in case anything changes. He coughs and follows up with a groan and grimace combination.

'Peachy. The cavalry is on the way. Get the bitch.' He snarls a little giving a level of anger to his words. He points with his head, urging me to get back in there.

'They better hurry the fuck up.' I stand up and, taking a deep breath, cross the small courtyard to the doorway. If I seem a little less than enthusiastic it is because I have already been inside and know what is waiting for me. At the doorway I stub my toe on a bright red fire extinguisher, you know, the inconspicuous kind. I must have knocked it over in my escape moments ago. I manage to keep the swear word behind my lips but I notice a black one and a blue one too. I know the black one is carbon dioxide, having set one off in school as a dare. It has an explosion hazard sticker on the side.

'Come out, you have stabbed a police officer and there are more on the way.' I wonder if that will work, she might surrender. A demonic face coalesces in the purple hued smoke, a soundless snarl forming on its face. I am taking that as a no. I pull the vial of Holy Water from my pocket and find it has broken and the contents are soaked into my jacket. Bugger.

Chapter 36

I am not of the faint hearted brigade but I am not going to try and charge through demonic smoke to get at the witch within without some tools. It would be like turning up at a gunfight with a butter knife. A healthy regard for self preservation is how I would describe it, much better than being cowardly. When I need inspiration I find it comes in the form of words.

'Fuck. Fuck. Fuck.' I snarl as I look round for something, anything. The place is a workshop full of stuff that looks totally bloody useless, I have used the hammer that was lying about. A few craft knives and chisels scattered about but not much that will do much good. Like a demented springer spaniel I am spinning around looking and finding fuck all. The second bout of swearing is nearing the front of my lips as I start yanking drawers open in a fit of hope not expectation.

A cruel laugh rings in my head, was it the smoke demon or the witch? I have no idea but the red mist descends.

I used to have anger management issues as a

child, you know stomping off in the huff when getting beat at football, cricket, tennis, monopoly, tiddlywinks you know the thing. Bad loser and flash temper. The mocking tips me over the edge a rage so visceral that I haven't felt the like for decades. A taunting sound that destroys my ability to rationalise. I find myself roaring and charging towards the smoke face in the doorway, unarmed.

The ground comes up to meet me in a split second and the air filling my roar is expelled in an explosive cough. The stars spinning round my head like a cartoon character a result of my collision with the stone floor. I would like to go on record thanking the Factories Act and the Health and Safety Executive because they have just saved my life. Something they have been doing for workers all over the land for years. The red fire extinguisher, a requirement for workshops, had rolled into my path and tripped me up. Saving me from a fatal charge into the waiting arms of the demon.

I groan, the agony of my fall seeming to engulf my whole body. I now realise what the Doctor had meant when he said you really need a long period of convalescence after my flight from the battlements.

The pain is good for me this time as the taunting laugh ringing in my head is no longer having the effect she wants. I know I am hurt because I can't even summon an expletive; mentally or verbally. I sit up, and it was a stretch to get that far, and notice the knee of my trousers is shredded and the underneath is an interesting red colour.

A moment of light-headedness passes as I try to get my shit together. My hands are shaking like a post bender detox session and I can't really do much more than glare at the face in the smoke. The modern fibreglass cast has shredded the back of my hand just adding insult to injury and a bloody stain to the cotton underneath. The ringing in my ears subsides a little to be replaced with a whispering 'The Master is coming' over and over again, undulating in volume in pitch like a bad sample. The hysterical undertones of religious fervour playing a counterpoint to the message. The witch has lost it, if she ever had it. The face glaring back at me has that arrogant cast that just gets on my nerves. I grunt as I get to my feet, it ain't over yet.

If I wait until the cavalry arrive there will be other casualties, policemen that are not equipped for this kind of situation. This one is mine to deal with; no one else's. I am leaning on a wooden rack still clueless and scanning for inspiration. The fire safety regulations for flammable chemicals, laminated, hangs by the doorway. Why would a jeweller have that posted so prominently? What chemicals do they use? I scan the room and see a chest-sized steel box, with stickers denoting hazards all over it, against the outside wall.

A painful, wincing and somewhat pathetic, few steps later I look inside to see bottles of dangerous chemicals and one I recognise. Acetone. It is perfect for my needs. I am going to burn the witch, medieval yes but with a modern twist. Fire consumes and purifies and has the added benefit of being my only option. The bottles are about the size of a wine bottle and perfect for throwing. I wont need a burning rag in the end. General Molotov would be so disappointed in me.

I throw the first into the face of the Smoke Demon, and it passes through leaving no sign of its passage. A second and a third are sent in the same direction. I don't have, what you might call, a good throwing arm and the third one smashes dramatically off the door frame. I throw the remaining bottles underarm, ensuring that they almost all get in. I can feel her uncertainty, as the voice in my head has stopped. She knows what I have thrown into her inner sanctum. If there isn't a bolt hole she is had it, and she knows it.

The Swan Vestas matches lying on the work bench strike easily and, resisting a quote from my favourite Christmas movie, I set the flame to the chemicals. The speeding aurora of flame seems to slide across the surface in a graceful wave heading for the grey smoke filling the doorway. The 'whoosh' sound as it gathers pace seems to suck the air before the bright flames start their consumption. I can hear the frantic activity from inside and know that there is no bolt hole. I move back, as the chemical heat starts to build, outside to wait for the cavalry. There is nothing left to do now.

'Master.' Her scream fills my head and my ears as she panics, the flames must be closing in on her. The power of her sanctum seems to have diminished in the flames, perhaps it has been cleansed too. I flop down beside DI White, he is still groaning a little. I smile at him, as a grim expression settles on his face, 'Better get a fire engine as well I think.' I wink at him.

'White to control. Fire service required on site. Workshop fire.' He presses the call button on the mic. I don't hear the response and neither does he as a concussive explosion blows out the windows and fills the courtyard with noise and debris. The screaming in my head is cut off as if a switch has been flicked. The shards of glass seem to land all round us and none find us. The flames are pouring out the windows and through the roof as the fire starts to eat everything that it can.

'Good luck putting that out.' DI White whispers, his lips beginning to look a little blue. The sound of the 7th Cavalry can be heard in the distance like a bad western. Well sirens, but unlike the cavalry they have missed the action and are arriving like British Rail, late.

'The building will be gutted by the time they get here. They'll be able to piss on it by then.' He needs to stay with me for just a little longer. 'You won't get a claim you know. Should have had your stab vest on.' I give him a nudge as the grin splits his face. The Ambulance swings in to view, thankfully. Some bloody cavalry.

Chapter 37

It is usually me that wakes up with some one else sitting in the seat watching. Tonight it is my turn. DI White has been lying inert for hours after the surgery. The stab wound was a little tricky apparently and luckily he didn't pull the dagger out at the scene or I would be sitting beside a coffin swigging his whisky. The ambulance guys were superb, no panic no fuss just a quick retrieval and blue lights all the way to the nearest hospital. I didn't know that Livingston even had a hospital but fortunately it did. The paramedic in the back was talking a stream of detail into his mic as we bounced along the farm road and so when we pulled up at the Accident and emergency door the whole NHS swat team took charge of my guy.

My patting his shoulder obviously helped as I tried to be there for White, the driver seemed to use the Edinburgh clock for our arrival time 'a few minutes' seems elastic around here. Anyway they whisked him inside and I was left to hobble after like a geriatric until a nice young nurse took care of my knee and the other scrapes. I should be thankful that the sticking plasters adorning my hands aren't smiley face ones. The paper stitches on my cheek make me look like a proper casualty. My knee is bound up with all sorts, looking much more impressive than a skinned knee has any right to look.

My mind is wandering like a vagabond tinker as I watch the steady rise and fall of his chest. The tubes leading in and out of him would worry anyone who doesn't frequent hospitals but I know what each one does. I have had some of them and I asked about the others. He is going to be all right , or so they keep telling me. I am waiting until his lights come back on before I am leaving. Is this how the Bishop feels when he waits for me? It feels awful. I feel myself alternating between reminiscence and tears. The memories not really about DI White but the peaks and troughs of my life and those around me.

'I bet the Bishop just reads the paper' I say aloud, quietly. And the happy sadness fills me for a moment. I shake myself like a dog coming out of a pond and know that too much thinking time is dangerous for me as the string of losses of the past tend to surface over and over.

I get up and totter round to read his chart for the tenth time in the last hour. I read it like a professional, flicking the pages and reading what is in the bags hanging on the stands. Waiting is murder. I pace quietly, like a tip-toeing tiger in a cage. The door opens and a middle-aged, matronly figure enters and tries hard not to glare at the muddy shambles standing at the end of the bed reading the charts.

'He won't be awake for another six hours or so.' She speaks quietly as she checks a variety of settings and writes on the chart which I have relinquished to her care. She checks him once more and makes sure he is as comfortable as he can be, even though he will never know. 'Go home and change, get some rest and come back in the morning. I will take care of him until then.' I wonder if she means you stink and are in the way but her eyes radiate kindness and an unexpected empathy. My stubborn refusal to leave evaporates as I accept that she is right.

I take his hand and whisper to him 'Don't die ya bastard. You don't have permission. I'll be back.' His eyelids flutter a little bringing a smile to my face. He's in there. I let him go for now, and let myself be ushered from his room.

Bright and early, clean and uncrumpled, I open the door to his room. The bag of grapes and three newspapers in one hand and Costa coffee in the other, I am prepared for a wait. He is still sleeping, I can tell by the small movement under the coverlets. I managed a few hours of sleep and the rejuvenation of the shower was like magic.

I feel like a weight of years has fallen away with the culmination of the case. For a little while the technicolour recollection of demonic murders will leave me alone as I sleep, until the next one.

I read his chart again, checking the times and events that took place while I was away. They are like clockwork and the initials beside each one telling of bag changes and medication must be of the Sister that sent me home. Funny how nurses are called Sister. I have a sister and she kept an eye on me loads of times, probably why the name has stuck for the group of women that have looked after others through the years.

I sit in the chair that, I hadn't noticed was uncomfortable last night, will be my guard post for the day. Time passes like dripping treacle, slow and dead slow. The newspapers, not worthy of the name, don't last long and the grapes last even less time as I pick and pick at them. The coffee a distant memory and the quiet passing of time draws me back to the case and what was going on. There was so much happening that the why has been lost in the noise, pain and deaths. I roll my mind back to the start and begin my search for the golden thread that will make some sense of the things that we have endured.

I can feel my face contorting to a heavy frown and frustrated crabbit mask as I trace the steps and cannot get it straight in my head. Why did she summon the demon in the first place? Why target young women with the jewellery? All through it 'the master is coming' is irritatingly replaying and interrupting. Father Jeremy will need to find out what that actually means because I have no idea. Something big is going on and I just don't know what. I almost growl at my lack of progress and I wonder how I explain to the Bishop that this one is over but a bigger wave is coming. The dark tide is rising.

I pick up the local paper, an early edition has our fire on the front page. A chemical accident and fire in a workshop resulting in the sad and untimely death of a jewellery designer. I feel my sneer develop as I read a story that says they know nothing but takes a few hundred words to say it. More inside will mean more guesswork and supposition. I turn to the page anyway. A picture of the cottage and an inset of the girl who died in the fire and more words detailing the tragedy. No mention of White or myself, so all good I suppose.

A moment, you know one that we sometimes miss, tells me to look again at the photo. I am looking but not really seeing the anomaly. Like an Escher or Rossarch dot splatter thing, I can't really see it at first but when I do it sticks out like a sore thumb. Standing on the hillside is a figure. It might be a local shepherd but I know it isn't. I can feel the malice emanate from him. 'I'll get you Matey.' I snarl to the paper. A cough from White calls me back to the room and I move to his side. His eyes slowly manage to open and focus on his surroundings. I am probably too close as he tries to see. His mouth moving a little, probably as dry as a sand shoe, and no words getting out.

'Good to have you back.' I smile to him as I get his water with the fat bendy straw. I feel the relief wash through me, utterly unexpected and I can feel my eyes a little moist. Luckily he doesn't notice as he drinks using all the energy he has to do just that. I remove the straw and watch his eyes close again. He will be back in a few minutes I expect.

'I ate your grapes,' I say quietly.

The End.

Printed in Great Britain
by Amazon